HORSES *of the* DAWN
THE ESCAPE

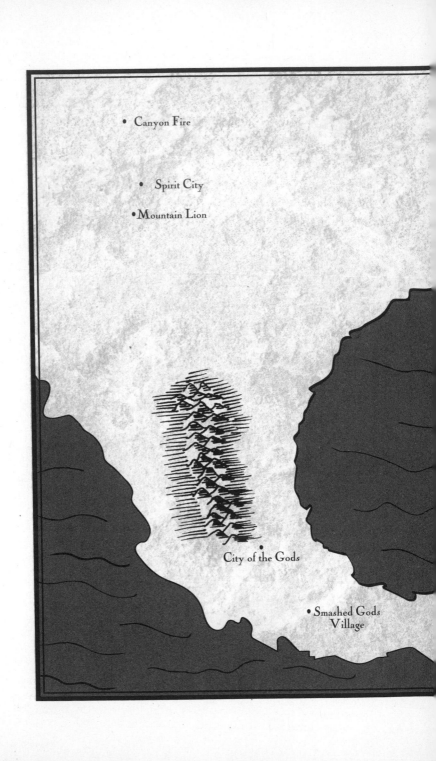

- Canyon Fire

- Spirit City

- Mountain Lion

City of the Gods

- Smashed Gods
  Village

N

Castolt
Island

First
Island

HORSES *of the* DAWN

THE ESCAPE

KATHRYN LASKY

SCHOLASTIC INC.

All rights reserved. Published by Scholastic Press, an imprint of Scholastic Inc., *Publishers since 1920*. SCHOLASTIC, SCHOLASTIC PRESS, and associated logos are trademarks and/or registered trademarks of Scholastic Inc.

No part of this publication may be reproduced, stored in a retrieval system, or transmitted in any form or by any means, electronic, mechanical, photocopying, recording, or otherwise, without written permission of the publisher. For information regarding permission, write to Scholastic Inc., Attention: Permissions Department, 557 Broadway, New York, NY 10012.

Library of Congress Cataloging-in-Publication Data

Lasky, Kathryn, author.
The escape / Kathryn Lasky. - First edition.
pages cm. — (Horses of the dawn ; 1)
Summary: Estrella is a filly, daughter of the lead mare, one of a shipment of horses bound for the new world, but when the ship is becalmed and the horses are dropped overboard to lighten the load, Estrella finds that it is up to her to lead the herd to land and safety.
ISBN 978-0-545-39716-2 (jacketed hardcover) 1. Horses — Juvenile fiction. 2. Mothers and daughters — Juvenile fiction. 3. Leadership — Juvenile fiction. 4. Responsibility — Juvenile fiction. 5. North America — History — Juvenile fiction. [1. Horses — Fiction. 2. North America — History — Fiction.] I. Title.
PZ10.3.L3773Es 2014
813.54 — dc23
2013037215

10 9 8 7 6 5 4 3 2 1   14 15 16 17 18

Printed in the U.S.A.   23
First edition, January 2014

The text type was set in Goudy Old Style.
Book design by Whitney Lyle

"Horses have a way of entering dreams and visions, even those of people who do not know exactly what they are dreaming about."

— Deanne Stillman

WATER

The Foal

The mare felt the foal shift inside her and kicked her leg in discomfort. The foal was coming soon, and the mare should have been on four legs instead of buried in a hold, hanging in a sling rocked by every wave the ship encountered. The mare should have been surrounded by straw or, better yet, soft grass in a meadow. *What a place to be born!* she thought. *A pitching ship in the middle of a sea!* The mare could sense the restlessness of the other horses around her. They knew what was about to happen.

The beam of the ship was wide, and ahead of her she could see at least eight other horses, ears twitching. The smaller animals — the goats and the pigs — were in separate stalls and out of sight. But it was the horses the mare cared about. She could see their ears flick forward, listening for the men, and then pivot back to her to hear if the birth had started.

They were in the mid-deck hold, near the pillars of the brigantine's two masts. Their stalls were padded with bales of straw so the horses wouldn't be injured when their slings swung too violently. The mare looked down at her legs hanging uselessly in the shadows. Her hooves barely touched the floorboards.

The mid deck was sweltering. Breezes couldn't reach the hold and there was little light. The horses couldn't sense the time of day. It was never bright nor completely dark; there was only shadow and a perpetual dimness that was not like any dawn or twilight the mare had ever known.

The last time she had foaled, it had been in a stall on land — dry, unmovable land — and the time before that, in a meadow. It was of course the best place of all to give birth. She remembered that colt well. His coat was beautiful, dappled like a herd of small moons sliding behind clouds. She called him Sombra Luna, Shadow Moon. And now another was on its way. Was it possible, she wondered, that the Seeker and his men did not know? She herself had been surprised. She thought she was much too old to foal. But surely they had seen her belly when they fitted the sling around her on the day before the voyage began from First Island. No one had said anything, but perhaps they were anticipating a short trip and the distances had turned out to be greater than they'd thought. She'd heard the blacksmith and the groom talking about how long the voyage was taking. The groom was just a boy, as gawky as the foal soon to be born.

She felt a sudden wrenching pain and gasped. The young

groom leapt from his hammock and rushed to her stall. The ocean had grown a bit calmer, but the mare's sling swayed back and forth in a disconcerting rhythm. The groom stroked her head. Then his eyes fell upon the large stain that was spreading rapidly through the canvas of the sling.

"¡Dios mío!" he screeched.

Within seconds the blacksmith was there with another groom.

"It can't be!" the blacksmith exclaimed.

It is! the mare thought. She gave him a withering gaze. The young groom's eyes had fastened on a small wooden carving of a woman with a darkly stained face, her hands pressed together in prayer. His mouth moved as if he were speaking to her.

"Don't pray to the Virgin, foolish boy. Get the doctor!" the blacksmith ordered.

Who's foolish? thought the mare. *All of you!* The men had been all too obsessed with their dreams of gold to see that the old mare could be in foal.

The doctor came. The sling was lowered and the stall was quickly banked with more straw bales.

"¡Calma! ¡Calma!" the blacksmith whispered.

Was he telling *her* to be calm, or the sea? the mare wondered. She hoped it was the sea. Giving birth was hard enough on dry land, and the ocean seemed to be growing more boisterous. But she could take care of herself. What troubled her was the thought of her foal being born in the hold and confined to a sling. How would a foal ever learn to stand on this swelling sea? She groaned deeply and her eyes rolled back in her head. She could hear the groom praying. But the blacksmith and the doctor remained silent as they removed the sling and helped her lie down against the bales of straw.

Time passed, but the mare couldn't tell how much. The perpetual half-light in the hold hardly changed from morning to afternoon to night. She felt the doctor and the blacksmith both pulling. The front legs were halfway out. One more pull? No, two.

"A filly!" the blacksmith finally said. "And so quick!"

"She's foaled before," the doctor said while clearing off the smooth white sac that covered the foal's body.

The mare turned her head and began licking her newborn's face. As she licked the foal's face clean, she saw a lovely white mark emerge on its pale forehead. The mare nickered with soft delight.

"Look!" the groom exclaimed. "She's trying to stand already."

The little filly staggered onto her legs, which seemed to be longer than her body. Although she had given birth twice before, the mare could never get used to how long a foal's legs were. Even though the filly was smaller than her dam, her legs were almost as long.

The filly staggered a step and fell down, her legs in a scramble. "Too many legs!" her dam nickered. "You'll have time to sort them out. You'll see!"

But just then, the seas roughened. A straw bale tumbled and knocked the filly down on her next try at standing. She went into a rolling tumble.

"Get her in a sling. And the mare, too. Get Perlina in a sling," cried the blacksmith.

"And what do we call this one?" the older groom asked, nodding toward the filly.

"Jacinta!" said the tall man just arriving. He was the Seeker, the captain of the ship. He named the horses. "Let us give thanks for this blessing. Let us take it as a sign of good fortune, of grace and the merit of God. Let us pray." And then, despite the rolling of the ship, the men fell to their knees beneath the statue of the dark Virgin.

"Good fortune?" the mare muttered as she looked across at her filly. *We are in separate slings and they call that good fortune and grace of their God? How will my filly nurse? How will she learn to stand? And Jacinta!* she raged silently. *He names my foal after his mistress!*

"By my withers!" She whinnied now loudly and in protest. However, between the roar of the sea and the voices of the men — for the padre had now come down to lead them in prayer — no one heard her.

The mare looked over at her foal. The mark on the filly's forehead looked like a swirled star. And the mare knew, whatever the man called her filly, she would name the foal Estrella. "Estrella! I shall call you Estrella!" she nickered. The foal looked into her mother's huge dark eyes and seemed to understand. She had been named for something bright and luminous, something that existed beyond the dark, rank air of the hold.

CHAPTER 1

Drinking a Star

The men found a way for the filly to nurse. The young groom or the blacksmith would come and remove the filly from the sling, then bring her to her dam and hold her while she drank. "Steady there, Jacinta," they would say. "Easy, Perlina. Here comes your filly." They were nothing but gentle and kind. As the filly grew, it required both the young groom and the black-smith to steady her.

One time when she had been placed back in her sling, Estrella turned to her dam.

"Mamita. There is something I don't understand."

"What's that?" The mare realized early on that she had given birth to a very inquisitive foal. It seemed as if the more Estrella grew, the more questions she had. Many the mare did not know how to answer.

"I don't understand why they call me Jacinta when you call me Estrella."

"The Seeker named you Jacinta. Not me. He named you for his mistress! I named you for the star on your forehead. That's your true name."

That was the beginning of the questions that were the hardest to answer — What is a star? What is the sky? What is a meadow? The foal's questions never ceased.

In this hold without seasons, without day or night, the one measure of time for Perlina became how much her foal grew. She could see that the filly was larger. If Estrella were to stand instead of sway in her sling, she would have been much taller than on the day she had been born. When she was removed from the sling for nursing, Estrella had to duck quite a bit to reach the milk. The mare figured that at least the cycle of one moon had passed since the filly's birth.

The days were changing. The wind had died and an eerie hush fell on the ship as the seas grew flat. Only the cries of the seagulls or the occasional creak of the ship or flap of a sail cut the stillness. But the canvas was bereft of wind.

The silence of the ship bothered the mare most — the silence and the stillness, for nothing seemed to move. Even the sling barely moved now. The mare sometimes attempted to remember the feel of the ground under her hooves. She cast a glance at her foal. For all her questions, the filly never asked about running or galloping. She did not know such movement existed, and that made the mare sad. Estrella stood briefly to nurse, but she had never bucked or kicked up her heels or felt her black mane lift in the wind, and she had hardly taken any steps, let alone run. It was all so peculiar. And now even the nursing times had grown shorter as the water was rationed and the mare's milk had begun to dwindle.

Equally strange to the mare was that her filly had never seen the sky — not the blueness of the day nor the black of a night. Estrella's life had been the sling and the walls of the stall. Unlike her dam, the filly had never been put out to pasture to graze and watch the comings and goings of the night creatures — the badger, the fox, the swooping bat, the bush rat, the owl or the moth taking wing. Most of all, the filly had never stood in the long grass on a summer evening and witnessed the sliding spectacle of the stars as they rose and made their transit across the night. She'd never seen a bright moon sailing high overhead in all its wondrous shapes as it waxed and waned throughout its cycles.

Meadow life seemed so long ago, before the mare had crossed an ocean with the Seeker, before they had landed on First Island in the New World and then set sail again. The fields were not so different in this New World, nor was the sky, but the stars were arranged in a different way. Still, there was one star the mare could always find. It never seemed to move. And she had gotten used to the new stars. There was one cluster with five stars that resembled a pattern like the cross the padre wore against his black clothes.

The mare kicked out with her back legs. Her filly should be able to buck, instead of lie helpless in a sling as the ship bucked.

Foals bucked almost as soon as they stood. That was what being a young horse was all about. One couldn't buck when one carried a rider. That would bring the crop down on the withers fast and sharp! But without a saddle, without a bridle — oh, how it felt to be free of the weight! One had to buck for the sheer joy of it. A young horse wasn't broken for riding for months. While they were free from saddle, bit, and rider, they could buck all they wanted, and they wanted to buck a lot. It was good for them. It helped them grow, gave them strength.

Sometimes, Perlina had frightening dreams about her filly. She dreamed that Estrella's legs withered away, hanging like little dead twigs from her body. She stole a glance at her filly's legs. Were they shrinking before her eyes?

The mare tried to explain the world to Estrella, tried to tell her of the sky with its stars sparkling in the night, and the land and open meadows. Soon, Estrella began to pester her dam for star stories.

"What do you mean, 'twinkle'?" she would ask.

How do I explain the twinkle of a star to one who has never seen the night sky? her dam thought.

"It's a little bit of light that shows up suddenly in the darkness of the night." But of course the filly only knew the shadows of the hold. Without dark, it was hard to know light, and without light, it was hard to imagine the pitch-blackness of the night.

Still, the filly was particularly excited about the star pictures that her dam sometimes described.

"There's a star picture that looks like us? A horse! Really?" the filly asked.

"Really." The mare hesitated. "Well, with one small difference."

"What's that?"

"It has wings."

"Mamita, are you loco? Wings like the birds you told me about? The ones we hear up there?" She tossed her finely shaped head up.

"Yes, but on a star horse. It's not real."

"If it's not real, what can it do? You said when we get to land, I'll be able to run and jump. It can't do that."

"It's very helpful to the Seeker and the sailors. The star pictures can guide them across the oceans."

The filly seemed to think for a long time before she tossed her dark mane and asked another question. "Could it guide us?"

The question shocked the mare. "Where are you planning to go?"

"I don't know, but could the stars guide us?"

"I suppose so." Perlina answered slowly, for she recalled how out in the pasture in the Old Land, the star that never moved seemed to hang directly over an ancient apple tree. "There is a star that never moves and you could use that as a guide — a guide star."

"How do you find that star?"

"Easy. You know when the groom comes and puts the water in our bucket how he takes that cup, a dipper? There's a star picture that looks like that, and the cup points directly toward the star that never moves. The men call it the North Star."

"North Star," the filly repeated softly. "Like my name. Estrella."

The mare extended her head from the sling to lick the filly's forehead. She so seldom got to touch her foal, so seldom got to run her lips along Estrella's pale coat. Only when the groom or the blacksmith came and released them from the slings at nursing time — and the times for nursing had become fewer and farther between as the mare's milk diminished. "I knew that your true name was Estrella as soon as you were born," she said proudly. "You can see the star on your forehead's reflection when they bring the water bucket, can't you?"

"Yes, but, Mamita, you don't have one. You have no star."

"Your sire did."

"They hardly ever bring the water bucket now. I might not see it again."

"Oh, you will! You will!" The mare tried to speak cheerfully and cover her fear. For in these long windless days, the supply of water was dwindling rapidly. If only it would rain.

Instead of the groom coming by three or four times a day to fill the buckets, they were lucky if he came twice a day. The horses' tongues had begun to swell and their mouths became scummy. Their lips were parched and cracked. Each time they heard the footsteps of the groom, the horses roused themselves and smacked their lips in anticipation. But a dull, lusterless light was creeping into their eyes, and the mare knew that soon, not even human footsteps would catch their attention.

"And your name?" the filly asked. "Why are you called Perlina?"

"For my coat. When I was born, the master said that I was the color of dark pearls, but my dam said I was truly the color of the light just before the dawn."

"I don't know the sky and I don't know pearls," the filly sighed. "Mamita, sometimes I feel so stupid."

"You aren't stupid!" the mare corrected. "You just haven't seen anything but the inside of this ship, this sling."

"So what are pearls?" Estrella asked.

"Jewels — decorations that the people wear." She paused for a moment. "But I don't think my coat is like decorations. I think my coat is more like the just before."

"The just before?" Estrella cocked her head. "I don't understand."

The mare closed her eyes and tried to remember what it had been like in those meadows where she had grazed in the early hours of the morning. How hard it was to try to describe the whole world. She began to speak slowly.

"The just before is a time of day very early in the morning. I don't know how to describe it exactly. If we were in a meadow, I could show you. But it is as if the darkness has grown tired. And it becomes dimmer and dimmer."

"That sounds sad — the just before."

"No! Not at all. It's when a new day is about to foal and sunshine is coming. There's the promise of the sun rising."

The filly sighed and looked about. "There aren't promises in here, are there, Mamita?"

Perlina was stunned. It was terrible to hear a young horse talk this way. She neighed urgently. "Listen to me, Estrella. There are still promises, even in dim light. The voyage will end. We shall get to land. You will run and buck."

"And see the sky?"

"Yes, and see the sky and the night and the stars for which you are named."

The filly wanted to believe her dam. Everything exciting seemed to happen out in a meadow where horses could graze. Estrella was not even sure what grazing was, but it sounded lovely. She had to believe her dam: The voyage would end. The sling would fade away like the darkness at the end of night. She would feel the earth under her hooves and stand in the long grass and even buck.

Still, despite her dam's promise, the filly couldn't help but wonder if she would ever see the open sky and a star like the one on her forehead. If only the boy would bring the water bucket more often, for they were all very thirsty.

Then, like a small miracle, the little groom did come and pour a bit of water into the bucket, filling it hardly a quarter full. But that was enough. A crack had opened up in the deck, and reflected in that scant bit of water were two stars! One was the white swirl on the filly's forehead, but the second danced like a silver splinter on the dark water.

"Mamita!" the filly neighed softly.

"What?"

Estrella delicately lowered her tongue into the bucket and lapped just a little. The silver was still there. "Mamita! I am drinking a star!"

Over the next few days, there was a phantom of a breeze, just a riffle of wind that licked the sails and then died away. Perlina could hear the crew swearing about something they called the doldrums. They cut the rations of grain and water again. The horses were not only thirsty now, but hungry as well. Their stomachs began to make loud rumbling noises and sometimes grating sounds as loud as the creaks of the ship as it lolled in this windless sea.

The priest prayed to his God for wind. The Seeker prayed for gold. But Perlina wanted nothing except water for herself and the filly. Her milk was drying up and she feared that soon it would disappear. She hadn't asked for a filly. She had thought she was too old to foal, but it had come. A little tawny miracle with a swirled star on her forehead, a black mane and tail, and bright stockings on her legs.

Perlina caught the faintest stir of wind that had made the brigantine creak and one sail flap languidly. But it was a taunt — within seconds, it had died away again. Yet for those seconds, that teasing wind brought something with it, a scent from the long ago. The mare knew that scent. It was the wind grass. She had never smelled that grass before, nor had she grazed on it, but there was something sweet in the smell that stirred in some long-buried part of her, the part of her linked to an ancient herd grazing at the beginning of time. The mare's nostrils flared and she tossed her mane. *Perhaps we are not sailing away*, she thought. *We are coming home!*

Perlina felt as if she had just gulped an entire bucket of water. One ear twitched forward and the other pivoted to the side. She neighed happily and the other horses turned toward her.

The Seeker's stallion, Centello, as arrogant as his master,

snorted. "Fool!" He was too stubborn to pay attention to anything except the commands of the Seeker.

But Gordo, a dappled gray stallion, fixed steady brown eyes on her. "What?" he croaked. "What is it, Perl . . ." His tongue was so thick in his mouth, he could not complete her name.

Perlina closed her eyes tight. She was seeing something, and the gray stallion sensed it. A landscape danced as if on the inside of her eyelids. There was a sea of grass blowing, and through this grass was a fleeting shape — that of a tiny horse. A horse that stood no bigger than a dog. But it was a horse. A perfect little horse.

Yes, she thought, *we are coming home!*

The other horses grew very still. They could tell the mare had felt something extraordinary. They dared not ask what, not yet. But a shiver ran through them, as if their deepest thirst were about to be slaked. There was something waiting for them, and only Perlina knew what. Freedom! A freedom like none of them had known for millions upon millions of years.

CHAPTER 2

"Estrella Is Her Name!"

The men's whispers lay on the still air like the buzz of flies. Perlina heard her name swim up through the hushed voices many times and then the filly's. She did not know what the sailors were speaking about. But she was nervous.

She tried to keep the image of the tiny horse alive in her mind. She felt as if she had to guard it. This was her secret and it was a secret that would appall the men. But suddenly, the Seeker appeared. His helmet was cradled in his elbow and he went to the dark stallion's sling to offer it to him. Perlina could smell the grain in the helmet, saved especially for Centello. The stallion was named for the jagged white marking that ran from his forehead to his muzzle like a bolt of lightning. He was always favored.

The other horses turned their heads, and their nostrils began to quiver. But Perlina turned toward the ship's hatch, still seeking out the other scent, the ancient one from the long ago. The scent of the tangy sweet grass, the scent of home, and the scent of freedom. Those three things braided together in her mind's eye. She felt as if she were teetering on a terrible brink — a primordial dream that was about to be realized or destroyed.

The grain in the Seeker's helmet smelled slightly of mold, but the stallion continued to eat. Then he slid his huge dark eyes toward Perlina as if to say, *See, I am the favored one*. Perlina wanted to say, *Favored for what? Old weeviled grain?* She swatted her tail and turned her attention back to the wind grass, so sweet in her mind's eye even though the breeze that brought it had died.

She wondered if her filly was hungry. It had been nearly two days since the groom had filled their bucket. Perlina knew she could stand to go without food, but with her own milk drying up, could the filly get enough nourishment? Did Estrella look smaller? The lack of water and food seemed to have shrunk her. She was not the size of a meadow foal, and her skin looked loose, as if it weren't quite part of her.

Then it struck Perlina. Not only had the young groom failed to fill the bucket, but he had not even visited them to pet them, rub their ears, all day. He hardly ever let an hour pass without coming to their slings to check for abrasions from the canvas or to smooth liniment on the patches where their coats had been rubbed bare. Where was he? She turned around to look for him. He was crouched in a corner as the blacksmith spoke to him. Wet tracks ran down his face. It was not perspiration but two parallel streams. Tears. The boy was crying.

"*Pero ella casi no pesa nada,*" the boy pleaded.

She doesn't weigh much? Perlina wondered. *What is he talking about?* The boy turned to look at the filly, and in that instant the image of the tiny horse faded from Perlina's mind. The scent of the sweet grass was replaced with a rank odor. She knew she was about to lose everything — her foal was her dream, freedom. Perlina let loose a shrill squeal and then an ear-piercing scream.

The filly had never seen her dam like this. She panicked and tried to buck in her sling.

The stallion looked over toward them and nickered through his closed mouth. He was safe, of course. The Seeker had just proved it to him by giving him grain. But Perlina's panic was becoming a fury.

"*¡Ella sabe! ¡Ella sabe!*" She knows! She knows! The blacksmith growled in a low voice. "*Es la más inteligente del grupo.* She's the smartest horse of them all. What a shame! What a shame! *¡Qué pena!*"

Seven sailors came down to the hold, carrying rope. Perlina squealed again and tried to buck out of her sling. She had heard rumors of *echadas*, or pitchings, and she knew exactly what was going to happen when she saw sailors wrapping the ropes onto the winches. Her eyes flashed to the muskets strapped to the sailors' waists. She also knew what would happen if she tried to resist. The sailors would think nothing of shooting her right here, then butchering her and feeding on her flesh.

"Horses are good swimmers," the blacksmith said, trying to console the boy. "Land is not that far. Remember that island this morning? It's a quarter league at the most. They could make it to shore. You'll see." He extended his hand and rubbed the boy's dark hair. "Perlina and Jacinta —"

"That's not her name. Don't call her that!" The boy's eyes were smoldering.

"Not her name?" The blacksmith opened his eyes with surprise. "What's her name?"

"Estrella — Estrella is her name!"

"How do you know that?"

"Her mama told me. It's her secret name for the filly, the true name," the boy insisted. He walked toward the terrified filly and began to scratch her ears. The filly and the boy locked eyes. *He knows my name*, the filly thought. *He knows my true name, the one my dam gave me. But what is all this talk about leagues? Why is Mamita screaming?* Estrella tossed her head wildly. Long silvery ropes of saliva from her mouth whipped through the air, but the boy helped to calm her a bit.

The hatches were opened. Estrella shut her eyes as a bolt of glaring sunlight fell into the hold. It was so bright she had to squint. The stallion Centello looked on calmly as the horses' slings were tightened. Perlina dared not give the stallion the slightest glance. She had to focus on trying to calm down, for she knew that her one task now was to concentrate on the filly.

With that first whiff of the sweet grass, Perlina had begun to see that they were heading to a more complicated world than she had ever imagined.

They were going home — but it was a home from the long ago, the place of ancient winds that blew through the oldest grasses. The Seeker had his dreams of gold. But what the mare had was not a dream; it was a history that ran through her blood. She and her filly were about to come full circle. If they survived.

Estrella heard a whinny and looked up to see the hooves of Gordo, the dapple gray stallion, floating above her on the winch. His shadow briefly slid across the patch of sunlight on the floorboards of the hold. Next she saw her dam's legs above her. What was happening? Perlina's parched voice nickered, "Don't worry! Stay calm! I'll wait for you."

Wait where? Estrella thought. None of it made any sense. Then she heard a splash and the scream of a horse.

Estrella kicked out and tried to twist away, but soon her sling was lifted into the air. Her hooves pawed at nothingness, and below her came a mad yapping. The Seeker's dogs! War dogs, mastiffs, and wolfhounds. Vicious creatures, her dam had told her, used for tracking and also attacking. The war dogs were running wildly on the deck, excited by the spectacle of the horses being lifted out of the hold. Their tongues hung out, as if to savor the sight. A mastiff barked and leapt up, trying to nip at Estrella's legs as they hung over the deck. The boy slapped him and the dog skulked off, but Estrella whinnied in panic. Where was her dam? Estrella's eyes swept the ship from bow to stern.

Suddenly, the deck beneath her disappeared and she swung out over the water. Her legs churned in panic. There was a click as her sling released and it seemed as if her stomach dropped out of her. She spun through the air, everything flipped upside down. Which was the sky? Which was the water? The screams of panicked horses laced the air. Estrella felt a loud, cold smack and then a sucking feeling. Storms of white frothy bubbles swirled around her. She couldn't see and began to open her mouth to scream for her dam, but water rushed in, gagging her. She couldn't breathe. Which way to air? Which way was up?

Her legs churned, but everything was a jumble. Sharp hooves lashed the water around her. She clamped her mouth shut tighter and pawed with her feet. Her muzzle broke through the surface and Estrella took in a wet suck of air. And miraculously, there was her dam. Right beside her!

CHAPTER 3

The Shadow in the Flash

"Breathe!" her dam commanded. "Keep swimming. And keep your head high!" *High and proud*, Perlina wanted to add, *for we are free!* But the dam knew she must save her breath.

They had broken through the surface. After the tumult of the plunge, the gasping for air, the boiling bubbles blinding them, the horses had emerged into a morning — a morning so full of the light they had not seen for so long that they had to squint. There was a peculiar stillness. The ship was not far away, but the vastness of this new world of light and water and sky had swallowed the creaks of the brigantine, the flap of the sails, the chatter of the crew. The sea was glossy and reflected the sky, the scudding clouds, and the scattered shards of sunlight. Estrella and her dam were floating in a crystalline world.

Perlina nickered to remind Estrella to stay by her side.

The mare swung her head and breathed in deeply. "This way. There's an island ahead. Not far."

Yes, land is near, she thought. And beyond the island was more land. The scent of the sweet grass flooded her nostrils, and the form of the tiny horse returned to her mind's eye. They would have to travel far, but she had no doubt they could reach him. They were strong and would become stronger every day. Horse strong, with no whips and no spurs to urge them on. "Try not to swallow the water." Perlina turned to her filly. "It's salty and will swell you."

Estrella clamped her mouth shut and lifted her head. She turned to look back. The ship and the clouds were perfectly reflected in the gleaming smoothness of the sea. She could even see the groom's face, for the boy had hoisted himself high onto the bulwarks and was clinging to a shroud. "*¡Hasta luego! ¡Buen viaje! Te amo, pequeña* Estrella." I love you, little star, he shouted. And the sound was sweet in the filly's ears.

The filly turned and lifted her head higher to better see the boy. Suddenly, his face contorted into a horrible mask. He opened his mouth wide, but no scream came out. Then one word tore through the placid blueness of the day. "*¡Tiburón!*"

Something sliced through the sea toward them. It looked like one of the blades that the blacksmith used, but much bigger. It was coming straight at them and fast, knifing through the glossy sea.

"Shark! Shark!" The sailors hung over the side of the rail screaming. The fat padre waved his hands, making a sign, and in his high shrill voice called out frantically to something in the sky above. "*Oh, Señor, Dios todopoderoso, nuestro Redentor, debe ser nacido en un establo y acostó en un pesebre cerca de donde estaban los caballos. El nombre del hijo de tinta bendiga estos caballos.*" But the filly could not understand a single word.

She felt something move beneath her hooves and whipped her head down to see what was in the water beneath her. Something white seemed to swell toward her, so vast and so white that it blotted out the blue of the sea. It rose up, ghostly and unstoppable, the water churning, the reflections of the sky gyrating until the clouds were spinning. Then there was an immense mouth and two rows of teeth, huge teeth like white daggers.

The horses squealed and bucked, as if trying to lift themselves out of the water. Estrella and her dam were a short distance from the others. The shark had caught sight of them — smaller, easier prey than the four horses swimming close together. He circled around and swam straight at them, almost slowly but inexorably. He was huge and Estrella could see his flat eyes with a dumb brutality as he brushed past her. He circled again, and then again, with each circle drawing closer. He rolled over on his side as if eyeing them.

Perlina and Estrella swam desperately toward the other horses, but there was no escape. The shark swept in and bumped Estrella. Perlina gave a frantic shriek and wheeled about in the water, forcing her bulk between the shark and her foal. Estrella screamed in horror, and the shark rose up and caught her dam in his teeth. *This cannot be!* she thought as her dam began to sink.

"No!" she screamed. Her dam's head tilted, blood foamed from her mouth, and the sea turned a deep red around her. But a light in Perlina's dark eyes flashed and a scent came to the filly — not of blood but of the sweet green of the wind grass. The image in front of Estrella's eyes shifted from death to the imprint of a tiny fleet creature running across a windswept plain. But then the image blinked away and the horror filled her again.

"No! No! No!" Estrella screamed again and again. She dove under the water to try and follow her dam, who was sinking fast.

The shark turned and knifed toward the filly. She bared her teeth and tried to shriek at him, but no sound came out. Estrella gathered all her strength and twisted around to kick out with her back legs, her most powerful legs. She connected with the shark's broad snout. There was a raspy sensation, as if she had rubbed against something rough. The shark seemed to flinch and his eyes rolled back. But she could not have hurt him. Her most powerful kick was still so light. Perhaps it was like when her dam had bruised a flank in the sling one night. Perlina had told her filly that the flank was a horse's most tender part. Perhaps the nose of this monster was tender, too.

The shark turned and swam toward two other horses, both mares. One was panicking and swallowing water; the other was trying to push her companion ahead. Then the shark swung around and dove for the quickly sinking body of Perlina. The filly was paralyzed in the water. The large dapple gray stallion pushed her with his head. "Go! Swim!" he shouted.

Estrella was almost numb as she swam away, feeling closer to her dam than ever before. It was as if she were filled with the mare, with her memory, her knowledge. She kept her eyes on the haunches of the large stallion swimming ahead of her. A colt swam beside him, mewling. She could hear his anguished whinnies. But Estrella kept silent. It was as if something had been sealed up inside of her. Her cries, her grief. In that profound internal silence, one image eclipsed everything. The flash in her dam's eyes, a single flash.

The light of it had not been blinding, but it illuminated the deepest recesses of Estrella's being. As if a long-forgotten history had began to unfurl in some part of the filly's mind. There was the now. There was the future. And there was the long ago. For Estrella, all three were woven into one seamless cloth. The filly knew somewhere deep inside her that she was the keeper of this precious cloth.

She looked around. The horses were confused, swimming backward and forward in a panic. Estrella raised her head again and sniffed the air. She would find the scent of the sweet grass again and it would lead her. Her dam was gone, her heart was breaking, and yet something of her dam was still with her. Something was driving her forward. She began swimming faster, passing the stallion. *Mamita*, she thought. *I never ran, I never bucked. You were so worried, but look! I am swimming, swimming fast.*

She whinnied, "Follow me! Follow me!" There was an island ahead, she could tell. First they must reach that island and then, though she could not explain it, they had to find their way to where the sweet grass grew. They must go back to where the first herd had run across the great plains. Would the others follow her? She almost didn't dare to turn around to look, but when she did, three heads bobbed behind her. The dapple gray stallion was nearly at her side.

Like a gossamer specter from an ancient place, the mare Perlina seemed to lead the filly, and the filly Estrella led the rest. She had been born but a short time ago. She had never galloped and she still could recall the taste of her dam's milk in her mouth. Yet right now she felt older than time.

The wind picked up and soon the waves were tossing up white swagged crests, like the manes of salt ponies skimming across the sea. One mountainous wave broke, sending up a fantastical eruption of ragged spume — pearl-white spume. To the filly, it felt for a fleeting second as if her dam were back. She could feel the mare's breath, sweet with the wind grass. Like a ghost horse, the spindrift whipped across the water. Overhead in the bluest of skies, clouds raced like an ancient herd coming home at last.

"¡Adelante! ¡Adelante! Onward, swim on!" the filly whinnied.

And the four surviving horses did. Their long eyelashes were encrusted with salt crystals. Occasionally, they swallowed a mouthful of water and began to choke. Estrella felt her legs weaken, but she kept churning forward. She knew she had no choice. The image of her dam in the shark's mouth flashed before her, and she kicked harder. The image of a tiny horse racing through a windswept grassland flickered brightly in her mind.

One of the older mares began to tire and sink lower in the water, her head barely above the surface.

"Vivi! Vieja! You can do it!" said the mare next to her, nudging the old mare on. "You are a royal horse, a horse of the court. You carried a queen, a prince. Your bloodlines go back to the Barbs. You have been bred for not just elegance but endurance. Endure!"

The old mare swam on, slowly, but with more strength. The words of her friend seemed to help.

Estrella heard the colt panting beside her. He, too, was tiring and beginning to fall back. What could she say to him?

Had he been in a court, a royal — what was it? She turned to the colt.

"Just try . . . keep trying. It's not far now. Look, you can see the island."

And it was not long after that their hooves touched bottom.

"So this is land!" Estrella gasped as she staggered from the surf onto the beach and collapsed. They all did. They were exhausted, exhausted and with a powerful thirst. Their tongues were coated with salt; their eyes stung.

"Water!" the colt gasped.

As the sun dried the large stallion's coat, the salt crusts on his body turned him nearly white. He lay on his side breathing heavily, his eyes closed and his tongue hanging out. A small crab skittered over it and he didn't seem to notice. But then he stirred and croaked a few words. "There's fresh water here. Not far." He made a dim motion with his head toward a grove of trees at the edge of the beach. One by one, the horses roused themselves and moved toward the trees. They drank deeply from the stream there, then collapsed on its banks, too tired to walk farther.

The horses lay under a fringe of broad palm fronds for a long time, and some slept. As Estrella's eyes opened, she saw, for the first time, the light change. When they swam ashore, it had been nearly noon — the time of the short shadows. But when she woke briefly during her nap, she noticed that the shadows had lengthened. *Long shadows*, she thought, and remembered that her dam had told her how the shadows would change in the meadow as the sun slipped lower in the sky. Now as she stood, she saw that she cast a very long shadow. *My shadow*, she thought, *is as big as a stallion!*

The colt was soon up and standing beside her. They were the first to recover. A few of the horses coughed in their sleep from the salt water they had accidentally swallowed. Their eyelids were puffy, but they were alive, which seemed miraculous.

Estrella and the colt took halting steps toward the deeper part of the creek. They drank and drank, and when they were full, they let their tongues loll in the cool water. Soon the three other horses came to join them. The one called Vivi walked to the center of the stream where the water was even deeper and crumpled to her knees, immersing her head for several seconds, then lifting it and spurting water from her nostrils. The other two horses followed and began rolling around in the muddy bottom.

Estrella and the colt looked at them curiously.

"What are you waiting for?" the stallion asked. "It's like bathing in a meadow pond!"

"I've never been in a meadow," Estrella replied.

"I think I have, once maybe." The colt spoke as if he were trying to recall a time from so long ago. But he was just a colt and most likely had spent only a very short time, perhaps until he was weaned, in any meadow.

The two mares came out of the stream, but the stallion remained splashing in the water. "I was born a dappled gray, not a salty white!" he muttered.

"There must be a corral around here someplace." Vivi looked about.

"Corral!" the stallion thundered, and then rushed up the bank, exploding from the water.

"Yes, a corral, Gordo. A *recinto*. Grain, water in buckets. Grooms to — to . . . groom us. Look at me! I'm all splattered with mud now that I got rid of the salt. It will dry and I'll need a good curry."

"A groom with a currycomb? That's what you want?" Gordo tossed his head. "Let me remind you, Vivi, a groom with a currycomb stood by while you were thrown overboard. And not only that, the padre said a blessing!" He paused and looked at Estrella. "It was men — grooms, priests, the Seeker, and his soldiers — who threw us over. They betrayed us."

"But they were good to us once," ventured the other mare.

"Once! Once means nothing!" the stallion rasped. The two mares hung their heads and said nothing, but the stallion was not finished.

"Once they curried you and braided ribbons in your manes for saint days. Once they put gilded saddles on our backs. But you know what?" He looked directly at the two mares. "Once doesn't count for anything! They valued that gilded saddle more than they valued you. Do you think they'd throw gold over the side if the ship wasn't going fast enough in the light winds? Never!" He lowered his voice and snuck a look at Estrella. "The men are responsible for Perlina's death."

Estrella's withers shuddered at the mention of her dam's name. She looked down at her hooves. It was then that it really struck her that here she was on land, unmoving land, where her dam so wanted her to be. It was here where she would learn to run, to buck. . . . Her dam said that she would not have to learn! She would just be able to do it!

In the name of her dam, she wanted to run, to gallop, to buck under the blue sky that she had longed to see. There were no more slings, no more stalls. She was free, but she was also alone. She would run as hard and as fast as she could and try to crush the grief that was crushing her. "Mamita, watch me!" she whispered, and she broke into a gallop down the beach, skirting the swags of foam from the lapping tide.

Everything was so different from the ship's hold where she had spent her entire life. She had never really experienced her weight on her own feet. Her tail flew out behind her, and air streamed past. The moon rolled up on the darkening horizon, casting a silver path across the water. The trembling light of newborn stars spangled the night.

Faster and faster Estrella ran until her front legs were just a blur devouring the land. Her heart was thumping in an insistent rhythm and something was singing down her bones, into her tendons and every fiber of her muscles. *I am horse, born to run! I am faster than the wind!*

She was not sure how far she had run. The beach was long, but soon she caught the sound of pounding hooves behind her.

"Jacinta!" the colt called.

She stopped short in her tracks and wheeled about. "No! That's not my name," Estrella said.

The other horses caught up with her.

"But that's what the men called you," Vivi said.

"Jacinta is what the Seeker named me!" Estrella said. "But my dam named me Estrella. And now we are here, like Gordo says — free of the Seeker, free of men. We need new names now that we are in this . . . this —" Estrella wasn't sure what to call this new place. She hesitated to call it a new world, because it was not. But would the other horses understand, did they also feel this sense of coming home? They had not seen that flash in her dam's eyes. They did not have the image of the tiny horse running through their minds.

"Name ourselves?" said the chestnut mare. "The men — they always called me Fea, Ugly, because of the spots on my muzzle."

"You are much more than the spots on your muzzle," said

Vivi, nuzzling the chestnut's flank. "They should call you Angela. When I was scared in the water, you kept saying you knew I could do it and you stayed by me. You reminded me that I had been a horse of the royal court who carried queens and princes on my back! You reminded me that I had a big chest and could swim. You gave me strength and — and courage. You were like the angel the old padre sometimes spoke of."

"Oh, but bless my withers, you were always so kind to me in the hold!" the chestnut mare said. "Not selfish like Centello. You shared everything. You are much more than just Vieja, Vivi, the Old One. In that big chest is a big heart."

"So we should call you Corazón," Estrella said.

"But they always called me the Old One, La Vieja. I'm not sure I can get used to this new name." The old mare cast an anxious look at her friend. La Vieja was a handsome horse. Her coat was a dark bay, but her hindquarters were white with scattered dark spots. It looked as if she carried a blanket of snow that had melted in patches, revealing swathes of her bay coat.

"Well, now we can call you Corazón for your big heart," Estrella said, and dipped her head. "With your permission."

"Yes . . . yes, Corazón," said the old mare, as if savoring the name in her mouth. "With my permission, call me Corazón."

"And me," said the old stallion. "They didn't call me old, though I am older than Corazón. They called me fat. Gordo."

"What would you like to be called?" Estrella asked.

"I'm not sure. I'd like to wait and see."

"See what?" the young colt asked.

"See if I find my name or if perhaps my name finds me."

The horses whinnied softly, as if chuckling.

"What will we call you while you wait?" Corazón asked.

"Hold On."

"*Espero?*" Estrella said.

"Yes, it's a nice word for waiting. I'm just holding on. I have patience; it comes with age."

"We could call you Paciencia," Angela replied.

"No," the old stallion said firmly. "I like Hold On."

"Then Hold On it is until you find your name or your name finds you," Angela said.

"I know what my name is!" the young colt whinnied happily.

"And what is that, Mitty?" Angela looked into his eyes. One was brown and one was blue, the blue one particularly striking against his black coat. It looked as if a piece of blue sky was peeping through the night. "I never understood why they called you Mitty," Estrella said.

"It was short for *mitad y mitad*. Half and half. For one eye blue and one brown. As if I am only half right. But I saw the reflection of my eyes in the water bucket on the ship and I love my blue eye."

"So should we call you Ojo Azul, Blue Eye?" Angela asked.

"No, no. Just call me Cielo, Sky. When we were swimming, I looked up and I saw the sky. It's the same color as my eye and it filled me up and made me whole."

"B-but, but . . ." Angela hesitated. "What if we meet up with our masters again and they call us by our names?"

"You mean their names for us," Hold On said rather sharply.

"Well, yes, their names. Don't you think it could be confusing, Gor — I mean, Hold On?"

"No! And put it out of your mind that we'll meet up with them again. We are on our own now. No masters! We'll figure things out for ourselves."

The two mares exchanged nervous glances.

Later that night, as the moon rose higher in a sky powdered with stars, the horses settled under the grove of palmettos by the stream. The shadows of the palm fronds splashed across the sand. It was the perfect refuge for them, with shade, shelter, fresh water. *But where do we go from here?* Estrella thought.

They must move on. She knew it deep in her bones, in her legs. The flash in her dam's eyes drove her. That tiny, flickering figure and the swirling scent of the sweet grass stirred something deep within her. She had proved to herself that she could run. Her legs were strong despite the endless days confined in the hold. And now something was waiting for her, for her and the four other horses as well, something that defied the power of men.

Estrella could not sleep. She missed the scent of her dam, and to succumb to sleep was to succumb to blood-swirled dreams and the terrible image of that knife slicing through the water. In the quiet of the night, there was nothing to distract her from the horrible images, and she grieved. She missed the pungent scent of her dam. The realization that her dam was gone seemed to course through her, and she gasped. Suddenly, the absence was raw, and sheer want overwhelmed her. The world seemed too big and there was a hole in it.

Some of Perlina's last words had been *Keep your head high*. But now Estrella felt as if she were drowning, swallowed by the void her mother had left. A panic surged within her and she gasped again for air. *I can't breathe!* she thought. She had not nursed from her dam for several days but now she missed the milk, even though it had been thin and watery at the end. She missed the sounds that came from deep inside her dam — the sound of her enormous heart beating, how gusts like the wind that once filled the ship's sails would stream through the bellows of her dam's chest. Estrella missed the smell of the stiff hair of Perlina's coat, and her sweat. Yes, her sweat. That was the smell of her dam.

Before the wind had disappeared to wherever winds go when they grow tired, the young groom and the blacksmith would gently take Estrella from her sling and steady her while she nursed. These had been her favorite times. Her mother was very quiet then. They were busy — the filly nursing, the dam trying to hold still for her. The blacksmith and the boy would lower her just a bit so she could set her legs on the planks and she would try her best to steady herself. And afterward, her dam would always say, "Estrella, this is the most important thing you can do now. You must drink my milk and grow strong. But it's easier nursing on land."

"Why?" Estrella had asked.

"Land doesn't move."

Now she was on land and she felt nothing but desolation and uncertainty. Yes, she had pounded down that beach and felt the sudden thrill as her hooves beat the earth. But for the filly, the rocking of the sea meant the smell of her dam. Motion meant the gentle knocking of her sling against Perlina's. The rhythm of her dam's heartbeat intertwined with the pitch and roll of the vast sea. Here there were no memories of her mother. Only the dry brush of the palmetto branches, the stars winking through their fronds, the quiet lap of the water on the beach. This was the world she was supposed to love, and yet . . . She laid back her ears.

A strange brew of fear and anger began to stir deep within her. She sensed it was dangerous to feel this way. To succumb to the terror and rage that felt like poison inside her. And yet they drew her in. *I want to die! I want to die now and forget the blood and the white shadow that took Mamita!*

However, slowly but surely, a scent began to thread through her grief. The filly stood up and lifted her head. She smelled the sweet grass on the verge of the wind. It was far away, on the edge of a new world she did not yet know. Somehow, her fear began to recede. She lifted her head higher. She could almost feel the beating of her dam's heart again. Everything was very still. The slight breeze dropped, but she could smell the grass in the distance.

The filly stretched her neck. Her ears softened and she moved them forward gently. She swished her tail slowly and felt the tension in her hindquarters dissolve. The filly stood quietly for a long time. Moonlight splashed down on her back. In the trees, she heard the chatter of night creatures. She looked straight up and saw one of the small creatures swinging through the treetops on the vines that fell like ropes. Hold On had called the creatures monkeys and said sometimes sailors kept them as pets. In the glitter of the moon, she saw the bright wings of a bird flying overhead. It was as if the ship's painter had taken a brush to the creature's feathers. And in the highest part of the tree were bursts of flowers that were suspended on the same vines from which the monkeys swung. A petal from one of the flowers floated to the ground, settling directly at Estrella's hooves. She bent down to smell it. It had a sweet, almost tangy fragrance, but she had no desire to taste it. She raised her head again and peered toward the treetops and thought how there was an entire world up there she did not know about. A secret world.

Estrella took deep, even breaths and felt a calm steal through her. The ground under her hooves felt good. Her legs felt solid; her muscles seemed to sense the earth she stood on. She let the stillness seep through her — through the horn of her hooves, the tendons of her legs.

You're ready for the new world, said Perlina's voice in her head. And with that, Estrella broke into a gallop.

CHAPTER 4

Forgetting

Estrella pounded down the moon-streaked beach. She heard her own heart beating fiercely now, harder than her dam's ever had beaten. The earth was once more a blur beneath her hooves. The voice wound through her head again. *You are the first herd, I the last herd, and we'll go forward together.*

Behind her came a heavy pounding and then a whinny.

"Hold on! *Espera!* Do as my name and hold on!" the stallion shouted.

Estrella slowed her pace. Foam dripped from her mouth and she smelled her own sweat. It was different from the sweat of the hold. It was sweat from running and not just from heat. She turned and saw the gray stallion picking his way down the beach.

Is that running? she wondered. His hooves struck the sand in an odd pattern, each leg lifting and striking the ground independently. It was quite pretty but not very swift.

"Why are you running that way?" the filly asked as Hold On approached.

"I'm not running. It's not even trotting or walking," he replied.

"What is it, then?"

"It's a gait for close combat. The *paso cierra de combate*."

"Where's the battle?"

"Nowhere." The stallion looked surprised. "I was taught that gait when I was a colt. That and so many others." Hold On began reeling off a half-dozen words: "The *andadura*, the *paso andado, marcha, el sobre paso*." His hooves began to dance in the sand, delicate little steps that looked silly to Estrella. "I guess I got used to them."

"Were they all used for close combat?"

"Oh, no. Most were to make our gaits smoother for the rider."

Estrella's dam had told her about being ridden. That was what masters did. They climbed onto horses' backs, but not before they had strapped on saddles and put something called bits in the horses' mouths. Estrella never quite understood what a bit was. It sounded horrible.

"How do they teach you these gaits?" she asked with a curl of her lip.

"Different ways. They hobble one leg to another with straps, or put strings with rattling balls around our legs. They use their spurs and bits."

"Bits sound awful!" said Estrella.

Hold On blinked at the filly. It seemed such a strange thing to say. He was so used to the bit, but of course it was awful. And of course the filly would think so. She had not yet been shod by the blacksmith. Her mouth, still soft, had never known the sharp tugs of the bit that gave such power to the rider.

Hold On looked at the filly steadily. Her resemblance to her dam was uncanny, despite the difference in their coats. Their eyes were nearly identical; he had noticed it immediately. Like her dam's, Estrella's eye color at first appeared to be brown with a touch of gold, like the deepest amber. But sometimes they seemed to glow as if there were a fire burning inside. Now in the moonlight, there was a spark in them that suggested a remarkable intelligence, an intelligence not unlike Perlina's.

The spirit of the mare lurked like a ghost horse deep within the filly. The old stallion made a quick decision. There was no need for Estrella to hear more about bits, nor about gaits and spurs. They were in a country without men, without riders. It was wild country and he must begin to disregard all he had learned in the Old Land. It would not help him here.

"Bits are awful. And I must forget my bit lessons," Hold On said.

Estrella cocked her head slightly to one side and regarded the stallion. Though he was dark gray, a few white hairs showed on his muzzle.

Suddenly, Hold On reared into the air, then plunged back

down again and thrust out his back legs. He began leaping and kicking. Estrella was astounded. She had never seen a horse move like this.

"It's bucking!" Hold On neighed when he saw her confusion. He was neighing and snorting and making all manner of boisterous noises. She could scarcely believe how high his hindquarters could kick.

"You're bucking the stars!" Estrella whinnied gleefully.

"I am bucking out the old!" Hold On shouted.

"The old gaits?" Estrella asked. His excitement was contagious and she pawed the air.

"The old everything!" he bellowed.

The noise woke the other horses and they came pounding down the beach in an odd array of gaits — the *paso cierra*, the *andadura*. She couldn't tell which was which. They all looked ridiculous to her and to Sky, as neither had been gait trained.

Soon, all the horses were bucking and galloping. Their antic shadows sprinted across the moon-washed sand. Sky simply flew. It seemed as if his four hooves didn't even touch the sand. But through the excitement, and even though the salt air swirled in her nostrils, Estrella kept her mind on the lingering smell of the sweet grass. She knew they must move on. The silvery path of the moon beckoned her, and Perlina's voice was like an ember in her brain. *You are the first herd, and I the last, and we'll go forward together.*

Sky galloped up to Estrella. "We're the fastest!" he crowed.

"It's because their legs still tangle in the old gaits," Estrella replied.

He flattened his ears. "Don't worry. They'll forget. Forgetting is good," the colt said. "I had a dam once, but I was weaned by the time they put me on the ship. I hardly remember her now."

Forgetting may be good, Estrella thought. She knew it would be easier if she could forget the death of her dam, but she steeled herself to remember. She had to keep the memory of her dam and the sweet grass firmly in her mind. She was of the first herd; she was the youngest of that herd and she could not forget, for she had very little memory of her dam.

She turned back and looked at the four horses behind her. Their strides were smoothing out and they gained speed and beauty. Their backs stretched and their strides lengthened as they shook off the old gaits. Their tails flared out behind them and their manes lifted in the wind, like spindrift off a cresting wave.

They know, Estrella thought. *They feel it. We are coming home.*

CHAPTER 5

The Sea Floor Rises

Just before dawn, the horses set off to explore the far side of the island. The beach ended abruptly in a point that projected out into a narrow channel. On the far side of the channel they could see land — a big land. The horses sniffed the air and blew, as they often did when they were curious. But what were they curious about? Estrella's ears pricked forward. Were they picking up the scent of the sweet grass? Sky's lips peeled back and his nostrils trembled slightly.

"Sky," she asked tentatively. "Do you smell something — something fresh and sweet?"

Sky looked at her quizzically. "No. I smell salt. Just salt."

"Nothing else?" Estrella asked.

"No." He shook his head, as if he regretted disappointing her.

Estrella felt that if they could detect even the faintest whiff of the sweet grass, it would bind them, make them fast as a herd. There were things that horses could not be told but must feel to accept. She could not tell the horses they were a herd now. They would not be a herd until they knew it, felt it in their bones. She was not sure why this was so. She just knew it.

Something more pressing concerned her at the moment. How would they cross the channel? The smell of the sweet grass led across it. But to swim again? To be torn apart by a shark?

Hold On trotted up and she turned to him.

"We have to cross."

Hold On looked at her. "Then we will cross."

"B-b-but what about . . ."

"Sharks?"

"Yes."

Hold On squinted. "It looks shallow. Not much deeper than we are tall."

"Is it too shallow for sharks? Shallow enough to walk across?"

Hold On thought for a minute. "Maybe soon. We should wait." He fixed her with a steady gaze. "You have someplace for us to go?"

Estrella felt a shiver pass through her. How could she share what she had seen in her dam's eyes? How could she explain a feeling or describe a scent? Hold On was not challenging her. His question was not one of doubt or defiance. Still, she knew he expected her to say something. He wasn't worried about where they were going, but he was very anxious about

Angela and Corazón, who seemed to want to cling to the old ways.

She turned to the others as they stood on the edge of the beach. "Sky and I have never held a bit in our mouths. We have never had a saddle strapped on our backs. We have never known the weight of carrying a queen, a prince, or a padre."

"But you could learn!" said Angela. "When they break you, you'll learn."

"We don't want to learn!" Sky snapped.

"Don't be rude," Hold On cautioned the colt. He took a step toward Angela and looked at her earnestly. "Do you really want these two to learn to take the bit? Bits can hurt, remember. Bits do not allow a horse to think." He said this very gently, as it was clear that Angela was agitated.

Estrella stepped beside him so her face was close to Angela. Estrella's breath stirred Angela's whiskers and the few salt crystals still clinging to them. "We don't want to learn the ways of the masters because there is something better waiting for us."

"There is?" Corazón came in close as well.

"Home," Estrella replied quietly. "Home."

Corazón looked puzzled. "You mean the home of the first Iber Jennets and the Barbs, our noble ancestors?" Corazón asked.

"Before that," Hold On said.

How does Hold On know? Estrella wondered.

"By my hoof, are you speaking of the ancient desert horses of Arabee?" Angela said with wonder.

"Long before that!" Estrella said, recalling once more the shadow of the creature that she had seen in her dam's eyes. "I'm talking about home. The place where the sweet grass grows and we can be what we were always meant to be."

Angela looked around, as if she dared not utter what she said next.

"Free?" she whispered.

Estrella, Sky, and Hold On nodded together.

"We'll wait," said Hold On, "until the water pulls back and it's shallow enough for us to cross this channel."

So they waited. All the horses except for Estrella and Hold On slipped into the posture of standing sleep. Their forelimb joints, the weight-bearing bones, engaged, and they locked in the joints in their hind legs by shifting their hips. Thus they were able to sleep comfortably while remaining on their feet. The last darkness of the evening faded and the world turned silvery. *It's the just before!* Estrella thought.

Her dam had been right. Perlina's coat was the lustrous color of those minutes just before the dawn. The pale, silvery gray enfolded Estrella, and the filly almost felt that she could nuzzle and nestle into the delicate shimmering light of a new day. She felt very calm. Just before the night leaked away into the first true brightness of the dawn, something caught her attention in the channel.

"Look!" Estrella said excitedly. "Something . . . something gold is breaking through the water!"

The other horses shook themselves awake.

"It's the sea floor rising," Corazón said.

"But earth isn't supposed to move!" Estrella protested.

"It's not," Hold On replied. "It's the water that's moving. Drawing away."

Estrella remembered that when she ran on the beach, the water had creeped higher and higher onto the sand. Now it was doing the opposite.

Low pink and lavender clouds skirted the horizon. They reminded her of the horses' tails streaming out when they had run down the beach.

"We can go," she nickered, and took the first steps onto the tongue of beach that stretched across what had been a watery channel. The others followed. The channel was not terribly wide and they started across it carefully.

A peculiar smell assaulted them as they walked into the water. The horses flattened their ears and snorted. There were dark forms half buried in the sand, and the horses could smell danger. Hold On seemed as nervous as Estrella was.

"They smell like death," he said. "But they're alive."

"What are they?" Estrella asked. She felt a rising dread inside, the same dread as when the white vastness appeared in the sea beneath her. One of the dark creatures ripped out of the sand and bellowed. His huge mouth opened, revealing rows of jagged teeth.

"Crocodiles!" Hold On shrieked. He had seen them on First Island in a swamp near a meadow. A newborn foal had been attacked and swallowed nearly whole.

"Turn back!" Angela cried. The colt skidded to a stop and trembled on his slender legs.

Estrella clamped her eyes shut and tried to fix the scent of the sweet grass in her mind. "We can't! We can't!" she said fiercely.

"Why not?" Corazón asked.

"We can't turn back now." Estrella's whole body was stiff with frustration. "It's just the very beginning."

Angela looked at her uncertainly. No one took a step forward.

Estrella took a shuddering breath and began to pick her way through the channel. The path before her seemed to squirm with the crocodile creatures.

Suddenly, Hold On was beside her.

"They caught our scent," Hold On said.

The strange creatures rose up on stubby little legs. They were squat to the ground, but they were big creatures, great in length from their flattish heads to the tips of their tails. They tossed their wicked heads as more and more caught the scent of the horses.

"We can outrun them," Estrella said. She could smell the other horses' fear. "Look at those stupid little legs. They'll never catch us! We can kick. We can jump." And then Estrella, who had never worn a saddle or held a bit in her mouth, suddenly knew exactly what to say. "We have no bits, no bridles. We are free to move."

"Estrella is right," Hold On said, his voice rising. "There is nothing to rein us in! We have full power." Then the stallion reared. "We are masterless."

Estrella paused to wait for the other horses to follow, but they remained standing where they were. *They won't follow unless I lead*, she thought. And she broke into a dead run.

She was like a low-flying buckskin cloud against the dawn. Her black mane and tail flared out like dark fire in the wind. When she hit the far side of the channel, she sprang over the first two creatures. The crocodiles bellowed and snapped at her with their huge mouths. The image of her dam's leg in the bloodied sea churned in her mind's eye. *No! No!* She leapt again, her legs curled tight against her belly as she sailed through the air.

The other horses ran after her. Squeals and bellows tore the air. The crocodiles scuttled out in all directions, dark bodies everywhere. Then suddenly, there was a cracking sound.

Like a whip! Hold On thought. *A training whip!* He jerked his head around. Streaks of blood splashed against the pink morning light. He wheeled.

"Sky!" Hold On screeched. It was Sky's blood that traced the air. One of the crocodile's tails had caught the colt and he was down. There was a blizzard of sand as the creatures rushed toward him, their enormous tails lashing the air. Sky scrambled to his feet and leapt straight up into the air. Hold On could see the glint of blood coursing down his black face.

Sky landed on the sand and kicked out into a flat gallop, sand billowing behind him.

"Sky?" Hold On asked as the colt reached the safety of the horses massed higher on the shore. A mask of blood covered the colt's face.

"I — I think . . ." His legs began to quiver. Corazón and Hold On pressed close on either side of him. "It — it — was the tail that got me." He shook his head, flinging drops of blood from his face. The blue eye shined through, bright as the morning sky. "My sky eye is fine!" the colt said with relief.

"What about your other eye?" Estrella asked.

"I'm not sure." There was a tremor in his voice.

Corazón began to gently lick the blood away.

"I think —" Corazón began.

"I can see! I can see out of it. I really can!"

"It's your eyelid that's torn, but I believe it will heal," Corazón said.

"Their tails — those creatures' tails. You can't believe it. It's good it was just my eyelid. They could have cut off my head with those tails."

"Look at them now. Just half buried on the beach. They look asleep." Angela sighed.

"Let's hope!" Corazón replied.

"We should go on," Estrella said, and started the long walk down the beach.

Had she known how many times she would say those words over the next hundred days, she would have been astonished. She would have perhaps been overcome with a paralyzing weariness and given up right then. But she didn't know, so the filly moved on and the colt, the two mares, and the stallion followed.

CHAPTER 6

Scarlet Feathers

The way was dense with vines, shadows, and trees — not just palmettos with their broad fronds but trees with enormous trunks the horses had never seen before. It was almost impossible for sunlight to filter down through the leafy canopy. Hold On had called it a jungle, but it reminded Estrella of the dim light of the hold on the brigantine, and it haunted her. She found some solace in the fact that at least she was standing on her four hooves and not suspended in a sling. But the going was tough.

Hold On had been watching Angela and Corazón as they picked their way through the thick vines. When Angela stumbled slightly, he called out, "Angela, you can't use that old *paso largo* gait."

"It's the fast parade gait."

Hold On snorted and tried to speak patiently. "You're not in a parade here. You're in a jungle! Don't do the ambling side gaits; just walk, pick up your feet high, and keep your head down so you can see where you're going."

"Hold On's right," Corazón said. "We don't have a bridle, a bit in our mouth, or a rider on our back with reins to guide us."

Angela stopped and shook her head slowly. "Are you saying I should watch the track myself?"

"Yes, Angela. Look where you're going, because there's no track here. We have to make it ourselves."

Although her first owner had named her Fea for the spots on her nose, Angela had been prized for her fine head, beautifully arched neck, and perfect throatlatch, the point on a horse where the windpipe meets the throat. She was considered to have the exemplary shape and lines of a horse of a distinguished lineage — an Iber Jennet. She had practiced tucking her head in and curling her neck so that her throatlatch became nearly invisible, as her master preferred. The only thing "*fea*" or "ugly" about her were the spots on her muzzle, which the royal stables always stained with dyes to cover up when Angela was on parade. "*¡Perfecto!*" the groom would say, and stand back from her, still holding his brush as he admired his artistry, the way a painter might admire a portrait he had just completed.

Not all spots were considered bad. It depended on where they were on a horse's body. Angela herself was a *pintado* with large splashes of white that floated across her dark bay coat. This was the highly prized spotting pattern known as *tobiano*.

Her friend Corazón had another kind of pattern, with much smaller spots that were more like swirls of cinders against her white coat. It almost appeared as if some of the cinders from Corazón's coat had landed on Angela's nose.

"Angela, don't worry about getting those pretty white socks of yours muddied in this jungle. It's the least of your problems," Hold On said.

How right he is, Angela thought, but wondered what her mistress in the Old Land would have said. She wondered if Semana Santa was approaching. Holy Week. Wasn't it getting to that time of the year? The ship had left after Navidad. She had been ridden down the street by the Seeker's very large mistress. Of course it had been nothing like the parades in Seville, and the Seeker's mistress was a poor rider. Her balance was terrible and Angela had to compensate for her bouncing about in the saddle, but she had finally found a gait to accommodate the woman. Thankfully! Angela's mouth was sore for days after. The lady's hand was as heavy as her bottom and she had constantly yanked the bit about. Angela should be thankful now, of course. This was the land of no bits, no saddles, no bridles.

But were she and Corazón too old for this land? It was one thing for young horses like Estrella and Sky to take on a new land, a new world. Youngsters would try anything. Then again, there was Hold On, no youngster and not a horse known to be impetuous. So why was he so eager for this masterless world? He spoke of freedom often. But did he not see that there were terrible risks in freedom — a horse might starve, for one thing. And she wondered if a horse could die from an unclean coat. Could one actually die for lack of currying?

So far, they'd been lucky. They'd found plenty to eat. And despite what Hold On said, Angela wasn't worried about her white socks getting muddy. But she did itch. She could feel armies of little fleas and critters crawling through the hairs of her coat. Nothing a good curry wouldn't solve. Oh, was there really anything better than the delicious teeth of a currycomb? The young groom was a natural when it came to currying. He had just the right touch.

"Bless my withers, he was good. That he was," she whispered distractedly to herself.

"Who was good at what?" Corazón flicked her ears. "Who are you talking about?"

"The little groom. Knew his way around a currycomb."

"Dream on," Corazón replied.

"I know it's impractical to wonder about these things, but, Corazón, do you ever think we'll feel the teeth of a currycomb again? You know the princess who owned me in the Old Land? Her father had curries specially made in the north. They were the best. They stimulated the oil in the skin and made my hair so soft."

"It is impractical," Corazón replied. "With freedom, many thoughts are impractical now."

"What a shame," Angela said with soft resignation. After a long pause, she spoke again. "You know, it's not that I don't like the idea of freedom. But I'll always miss some of my masters. And I like having impractical thoughts."

Corazón chuffed. "Well, you can still have them, dear. No rules against that."

The jungle was an alien landscape for all of them. On First Island, there had been jungle, but it had been macheted back to create fields and meadows. In the Old Land, the horses had seen forests, even been ridden by their masters through them, but forests were nothing like these jungles with the constant dripping from the thickets of palm fronds, and with dense, tangled vegetation that sometimes made the way almost impenetrable.

Walking was not easy, but they were learning slowly how to negotiate the mud, the entwining roots, the tight spaces. It scared them, for if they had to run, there was no clear path ahead. It was not like the beach, where Estrella had run until her heart was thumping and a melody seemed to sing down her bones and let her know there was nothing better than to be a horse — a horse born for speed.

They were adjusting to the noise — the harsh squawks of the parrots that swooped through the treetops and the chittering of the monkeys. It was a shadowy world, but now and then it erupted with small colorful spectacles — the flight of a luminous blue butterfly with wings as broad as a small bird, or a cascade of blossoms growing from the highest part of a tree. And always there was the constant *drip drip drip* of moisture falling from the broad fronds. The horses didn't see any grass to eat, but the leaves, although much less tender, were not bitter and satisfied their hunger. Water was no problem at all. There were small pools and they could always find water in a particular type of plant, which they began to call the bucket plant, for its leaves swirled up to form a small narrow tank they could lap from. Corazón especially loved the tender innermost leaves of the bucket plant and, after drinking the water, would munch on them.

As they traveled, two large birds began to fly over them with increasing curiosity. They seemed to have an uncanny ability to mimic the horses' nickers and snorts and neighs.

"Are they making fun of us?" Sky asked with an annoyed glance above.

"Why would they do that?" Estrella asked.

The birds were colorful creatures, splashed with red, blue, and yellow feathers.

"I'm not sure, but I think they might be royal!" Angela said.

"Royal?" Hold On asked in a bewildered tone. "Why would you ever say that?"

"Look at them!" Angela replied, tossing her head. "They're wearing the color red, the scarlet of the Royal House of Aragon. The same as the royal infanta wore on the occasion of her marriage to Don Jose de Castile, who was the second cousin once removed —"

"Angela, really now!" Hold On shook his head.

An echo seemed to buzz through the air. "Angela, really now!"

They all jumped.

"Who said that?" Corazón neighed.

"Who said that?" The two birds settled in a tree above them and flung the words back at them.

"It's them!" Angela reared.

Estrella and Sky were captivated. They'd only caught glimpses of the birds before, and now they could see them clearly. Estrella had never even seen a bird until she had been hoisted onto the deck of the brigantine where there were seagulls flapping in the sky. But these birds were entirely different.

"They're parrots," Hold On said. "They do that. I've been on many ships, and once a sailor had a parrot. He would carry it up into the rigging when he had to splice lines and halyards. They hardly ever stopped talking, not just mimicking like these two."

"You, big boy! Who says we just mimic? Big boy! Big boy! Big boy!" called the birds.

The chatty creatures swooped down from the canopy in dazzling splashes of color.

"If I didn't know better, I would think it was raining paint!" Corazón said.

"Or a rainbow come to life!" Angela said with wondrous delight as the two birds clattered about in the lattice of palm fronds.

"So those are parrots?" Sky said, staring in wonder.

"We're not parrots!" the two birds shrieked.

"What are you, then?" Hold On asked.

The two birds puffed up their plumage. The larger one, the female, squared her colorful shoulders.

"We are scarlet macaws," she replied with distinct pride.

"Scarlet!" sighed Angela. "I knew you were royal. Only royalty can wear scarlet."

The macaws exchanged glances. "Should you tell her or should I?" the male asked.

"Maybe you," the female replied with an odd look at Angela.

The macaw stepped forward. "We do not 'wear' scarlet. We are not robed. We are feathered! This is the way we are, the way we hatched."

"Well, not really," the female corrected. "When we hatched, we had hardly any feathers at all, Alfo."

"True." He paused. "When our plumage came in, these were the colors."

"But how did you learn to speak with us?" Angela asked.

"Oh, we can speak with anyone. My name is Lala, by the way, and this is Alfo," said the female. "We were bought by a sailor and then crossed the ocean with him."

"But it was not our first voyage," Alfo said. "Oh, no. We've had many, many voyages. Many languages. Time in the hold with the horses, time in the mess with the sailors. Talk talk talk. Couldn't help but pick up a word here, a word there."

"We love to talk almost as much as to fly," Lala added. "But I suppose Alfo just proved that."

"Do you know how much farther until open country?" Estrella asked.

"Not sure, really," Alfo said. "We prefer jungle. But we have to go now."

"Must you?" Estrella asked. She had been rather enjoying the conversation.

"Yes. It's nut time," Lala said. "Big wonderful nuts back near the beach. We love nuts, and if we don't get there quickly, other macaws and parrots will." There was a sneer in her voice when she said "parrots." "They'll wipe them all out until next season."

As soon as the macaws left, Estrella missed them. She had never met a scarlet macaw. That evening, Sky was lapping up water from a bucket plant when he jumped straight into the air and whinnied.

"By my hoof!" Sky had taken to some of the favorite curses of the older horses.

"What is it?"

"I think, I think . . . I drank — I swallowed one of those tiny crocodiles!"

"They are not crocodiles," Corazón said. "They are little lizards. They scampered all over the master's villa on First Island. Nothing to fear."

"It's tickling the inside of my stomach!"

"That's your imagination, dear," Angela said. "It would be dead by now."

"And that's supposed to make me feel better?"

"You'll get rid of it sooner or later," Hold On said.

"Can we not discuss such things?" Angela snipped.

But suddenly the mare started bellowing.

"What is it?" Estrella asked.

"I've lost a shoe! A shoe! This wretched mud has sucked it right off! How will I go on without my shoe?"

Hold On snorted. "You will go on very well indeed. Especially when you lose the other three!"

"We don't have shoes, Estrella and I," Sky offered more kindly. "We don't miss them a bit."

"How can you miss what you've never had?" Angela said grumpily. The two young horses looked at each other, uncertain how to answer.

Hold On stepped forward, whisking his tail. He looked into the mare's eyes and began to run his teeth softly through her withers to groom her. "You should be congratulated, Angela," he said between strokes. "You are the first to lose a shoe in the New World. It is an achievement! You watch — when you lose the other three, you will be able to feel the earth better, travel more easily. You will become so fleet."

"But, Hold On," Angela whispered, her voice tremulous, "I'm scared. Really scared."

"I know, dear, but things will be better."

"I hope." She paused, almost as if she were confessing. "You know, I loved my mistress, the infanta."

"But look. She let the Seeker buy you from her father," Hold On reminded her gently.

"She didn't have much choice. The family had wanted the Seeker to go, to find gold."

"Gold — that's all they care about! And what will he tell the infanta when he returns with chests of gold but not her favorite horse?"

Angela looked up pleadingly. "She never called me Fea, Hold On. She didn't think I was ugly at all. She thought I was beautiful."

"What did she call you?" Hold On said, still grooming her. Angela closed her eyes and sighed as if she were recalling the sound of her mistress's voice.

"Come on, tell me," Hold On encouraged.

"Promise not to laugh?"

"I promise."

Angela lowered her eyes shyly. "She called me Gatita."

"Gatita?" Hold On was confused. "But that means —"

"I know what it means. 'Kitten.' She said the spots on my muzzle reminded her of a soft little kitty she had once."

Hold On was not tempted to laugh in the least. He thought it was sad, terribly sad, to name a beautiful horse for a cat. A mare who, despite the spots on her nose, had the blood of the noble desert horses running through her.

"You will be fine without that shoe, Angela," Hold On said. "I envy you. I can't wait to lose one myself."

"I hope you're not just saying that, Hold On."

"I mean what I say." And then he thought to himself, *Although I might not always say what I mean!* What he felt about the infanta's name for this noble horse was best not said.

The very next day, Hold On lost a shoe and then, by evening, another. The mud sucked off their shoes faster than they could imagine.

They continued on through the dense jungle for what seemed an endless time, and as they traveled, they passed several lagoons where they saw more of the strange and horrible creatures who had attacked them on the beach. The horses were very careful when they stopped to drink at the freshwater pools where the creatures lay just beneath the surface, only the bumps of their enormous eyes poking through. The horses learned that the crocodiles were as afraid of them as they were of the crocs. Hold On, as the largest, took to stomping and squealing and even screaming as they approached each lagoon. This storm of horse noises seemed to keep crocodiles at bay while the horses drank.

There was plenty to eat in the jungle. Aside from the broad leaves, there were strange fruits they had never seen before. But search as they might, there were no grains to be found. The best part of the new food was that none of it had weevils, as Corazón pointed out while munching on a long yellow fruit.

"I ate my last weevil on that ship! Though this tastes odd, it's far superior to a weevil."

On perhaps the fourth or fifth night as they threaded their way through the jungle, they began to sense eyes watching them, tracking them almost constantly as they picked their way around the enormous trees. They listened carefully but never heard so much as a footstep.

"We're being stalked," Hold On said.

"By what?" Angela asked, her wide eyes rolling behind her. "I sense it, but I never hear it."

"Or smell it," Corazón added. "It's as if a shadow is tracking us."

Somehow, the less they knew about the creature, the more frightening it became in their minds. It was as if they lived in the constant shadow of a never-ending dread. Estrella could not help but think of that other shadow — the white one that had appeared in the sea and circled closer and closer. Whatever this creature was, it had to be more familiar with the jungle than they were. And if it decided to attack, where would they run? The vines closed in on the horses, blocking any escape. These thoughts were very much in all their minds when Hold On stopped walking. "We need our rest. We have to sleep, but not all at the same time."

"What are you saying?" Corazón asked.

"We must set a watch, just as the sailors do on the ship, so that some can sleep while the others tend to the sails."

"But we're horses," Angela said. "We've never had need for a watch."

"Because we've always been in a *recinto*, or a meadow that was fenced."

"Our masters protected us," Angela muttered.

"And now we're in a jungle where there are no masters," answered Hold On. "So we must become our own masters and watch out for one another."

Angela blinked and nodded. Hold On realized that she was beginning to understand.

"Might Corazón and I take the first watch?" Angela asked.

Hold On was elated. "Most definitely. Thank you, thank you so much!"

And so they set up a watch while they slept, and they traveled during the day in a tight pack.

As each day passed, they became more jittery.

"Why won't it come out?" Corazón said tensely. "If it would just show itself."

The horses were jumping at every shadow. No one was sleeping well and those on watch were tense and skittish.

It would be another two days before they glimpsed the tracker.

"There!" Estrella neighed softly and tossed her head toward a mass of gigantic roots that poked up from the ground like solid walls to support an enormous tree. A creature that looked like a cat but was many times larger stood frozen in front of one of the root walls.

Why? Why now is he showing himself? Estrella wondered. Was it like the shark who had circled and bumped her as if to test before striking?

Estrella understood why they had never seen the cat until he chose to reveal himself. The huge cat's pelt of golden fur was covered with dark spots that blended in with the shadows of the jungle. The pattern broke up the creature's form so that he could slip through the trees undetected.

"Stay together!" Estrella warned. She was not sure how she knew this — perhaps it was an instinct from the old herd, the last herd. The creature's tawny eyes followed them, as if daring one to lag behind.

"He'll eat nothing more than our shadows," Hold On said. And thus the creature was named Shadow Eater.

Over the course of the following day and night, the horses did stay together. They maintained their watches as the Shadow Eater continued to stalk them. The creature walked very softly, and yet they had learned to discern the sound of his huge paws on the jungle floor. His menace surrounded them with a terrible constancy.

"He never eats. He never sleeps," Sky whispered. "How can he do it?"

Estrella shook her head. "I don't know. I can't imagine."

During the scant time she had to sleep, Estrella began to have shark dreams, terrible dreams seeped with raw, silent violence. What disturbed her most was the whiteness of the shark and his utter silence. Most creatures squawked or whinnied or perhaps roared, but the shark — like the Shadow Eater — was completely mute.

Then one evening, it seemed as if the creature vanished. The next morning, there was still no sign of the Shadow Eater. And throughout the day and into the next, the horses began to wonder if the shadow had receded forever. They kept a watch, but they began to relax. Slowly, the terror left them, until, five days after the creature had disappeared, Corazón caught the sweet heavy fragrance of a bucket plant and wandered a short way off to follow it. Some bucket plants grew from the ground, but others, the sweetest ones, attached themselves to the trunks of trees. She was stretching toward one near the base of a tree when there was an explosion of spots and a terrible shriek.

Something slammed into Corazón's side and she collapsed to the ground. It took only seconds, but to the horse, it felt as though time had slowed.

Each moment dropped like small fragments into Corazón's mind. *I am down. The Shadow Eater is going to kill me. I feel his claws!* She rolled and kicked out desperately. The cat's fangs were near her face, near her neck, and she knew —

There was a loud clatter, and a rainbow shattered through the green canopy overhead. The jungle rattled with a clamorous squawking, and then the squawking was cut by a horrific shriek. Feathers of all colors spun through the dim light, and the Shadow Eater rolled off Corazón's body, blood coursing down its face.

Birds! The high-pitched, shrill screams of macaws and

73

parrots pierced the air like arrows. "Go for the the eyes! The eyes!" they shrieked.

The Shadow Eater raced away, his face a mask of blood. Corazón rolled to her feet and stood shivering. Miraculously, she'd suffered only a small cut on her shoulder where the Shadow Eater's claws had torn her skin.

Lala and Alfo and half a dozen other birds landed in front of the horses.

"You came back?" Estrella gasped.

"The nutting was no good. Then we got here and saw the jaguar stalking you."

"You were just in time," Hold On said.

"Just in time," Estrella whispered. She cocked her head and looked at the array of colorful birds, some perched on branches, others on fallen logs. There was a scattering of bright feathers on the ground. "Are you okay? Can you still fly?"

"Of course!" said a bright green parrot, who swooped down from a branch. "Most of us were close to molting as it was." The bird paused and looked hard at Estrella with her small beady eyes. "Look. This is the jungle. You are earthbound. You have none of the natural advantages we have. But you are twice as big as that jaguar and we're hardly bigger than one of his paws —"

Estrella broke in. "And you saved Corazón." The horses hung their heads in shame.

"Thank you . . . thank you . . ." Corazón's voice was ragged, her chest still heaving in panic.

"Don't thank us," said a scarlet macaw. "Learn to fight!"

"We — we —" Angela began to speak but could hardly muster the breath. "We carried our masters into battle sometimes. But they rode us. They guided us."

"Precisely!" the macaw said. "They rode you. We know about masters. Oh, yes, we know about masters."

Estrella peered down at the macaw, who was perched on a rotting log. "I don't understand how you did that. How you beat the jaguar off. You tore out his eyes!"

With a quick look at Estrella, the green parrot picked up a thick, sturdy branch in his beak and bit down. There was a loud crack and the branch broke in two. The horses were stunned.

"No one expects it," said a bird with beautiful turquoise and green feathers. "They just think we're pretty. But back in the Old Land, I broke out of my cage. A metal cage!"

"You're from the Old Land?" Angela asked.

"Some of us," Alfo replied. "Some not."

"Some of us have always been wild!" cawed a parrot.

"Wild." Hold On whispered the word. But Angela and Corazón looked at each other nervously.

CHAPTER 7

Uncaged

"We were not always wild, uncaged," Lala replied. "We had to learn." She turned her head toward Alfo.

"Learn what?" Estrella asked.

"To fly and to be wild," the birds answered at once.

"But you're birds!" Corazón exclaimed.

"We were birds with clipped wings, and with clipped wings we are not fully flighted," Lala replied. "It would be as if you were missing a hoof — you couldn't walk or run." She swiveled her head toward Angela. "When we first met, you spoke of royalty, my dear."

Angela nodded and shoved her ears forward with new interest.

"Alfo and I spent our early lives in the royal menagerie of the Duke of Cadiz. We became a gift to the captain of a ship from the duke. Of course, the understanding was that the captain would return with money. But on his return, not far out from land, the ship began to founder. They opened our cages to let us escape." Lala stopped now. It was as if she could not go on.

Alfo continued. "That was when we found out what it meant to be clipped. We could hardly fly the length of the ship with our primaries sheared off. How far can one go?"

"It wasn't just that they sheared our primaries. They clipped more on our port wing than our starboard, which meant that we flew unbalanced. We could only turn in one direction," Lala added.

"That seems even crueler," Hold On said. "It's as if they were tempting you with flight but punishing you for trying."

"Exactly!" said Alfo.

"How did you get away?" Estrella asked.

"The bosun," Alfo answered. "The man who tends the rigging on the ship. He rescued us."

"The ship started to sink and he scooped us back into our cage and took us in the lifeboat with him. We got back to land just fine, and shortly after, he found his way to a new ship."

"Still no smarter about birds," Alfo said. "He was a bit of a lazy fellow and didn't take the trouble to clip us."

"We could feel our feathers growing every day; it was quite wonderful. When the time was right, we would fly."

"We didn't even have to bite the metal to get out of the cage!" said Alfo. "On calm days, when the weather was good, the bosun would take us deckside and tether us to a winch pin."

"A winch pin?" Corazón said. "That sounds hard — anything with a tether sounds difficult to break away from. A tether is a rope, right?"

"We know ropes," Hold On said ominously.

"Ropes are nothing to us," Alfo replied, and picked up a large and very hard nut in his beak. With a sharp crack, he split the nut in two.

Lala sighed as if savoring the memory. "We were fully fledged. We were ready for flight. One clip of the beak, and we were free."

"It's . . . it's like when I ran on the beach. The first time," Estrella said. Her voice brimmed with excitement. "I had never set my legs on earth. I had been told I was a horse, but it wasn't until then that I felt it."

"And where are you going now on those fine legs of yours?" Lala asked. The four horses swung their heads toward Estrella, ears pricked.

Estrella swallowed. "There's a place far north, where the sweet grass grows. A green place with sweeping seas of grass and no people. A place where horses can run and be free. It's . . . it's yonder."

"Yonder." The other horses nodded and whispered the word. Estrella was filled with great excitement. The other horses may not have seen the flash in her dam's eyes, but somehow they were beginning to understand. She knew they were with her now, all the way to the sweet grass, to the yonder.

Alfo nodded and began to speak. His voice seemed to have lost its rasping edge. "You will discover, as you meet your true self, that you're not encountering a stranger. So there's nothing to learn," Alfo said. "When you find your true self, there are only things to unlearn."

"Unlearn," Angela whispered, and looked down at her hoof with the missing shoe.

Uncaged, Corazón thought.

And Estrella and Sky both wondered what a cage was like. A stall perhaps? A sling?

CHAPTER 8

Broken Gods

The macaws and the parrots soon departed in search of nut trees. The jungle seemed silent without the clatter of their flight and their noisy squawking.

On the evening of the following day, it began to drizzle softly. The vegetation had thinned considerably, save for an immense banyan tree. Hold On thought that perhaps they were finally coming out of the jungle and he picked up his pace.

Suddenly, he caught a scent that made him and the two mares nervous. It wasn't the heady fragrance of the jungle flowers, but a slightly metallic odor on the brink of rotting, mingled with something familiar.

"Horses!" Angela exclaimed.

Corazón inhaled deeply. "Grullo! My old friend Grullo!"

The two mares whinnied and broke into a gallop, tearing through a screen of vines that dripped from the banyan tree.

Hold On held up his head and peeled back his lips as if he were drinking in the night and the odious smell. There was something wrong. Under the scent of the Seeker's horses was the rotting, metallic smell. *Blood!* he thought. *Dead men.*

"Wait! Wait!" Hold On bellowed. "Fools!"

He wheeled on Estrella and Sky. "We have to get them before it's too late!"

Hold On, Estrella, and Sky streaked after the two mares. They caught up to them on the far side of a clearing where the mares stood stiff-legged and trembling. The jungle growth had been deliberately cut back here, and the ground was scraped bare except for a few large, broken stones that were wet with blood.

Hold On jumped sideways and screeched, and Sky began to stamp in place, his eyes bulging. Estrella felt a deep fear invade her.

There was blood, blood all around. She felt as if she were being dragged back to that white place in the middle of the sea, stained with the blood of her dam.

On one of the broken rocks, blood dripped down carvings of monstrous figures with faces like men and bodies like snakes or animals.

"Whose blood is this?" Hold On roared. They looked around wildly, but at first they saw nothing. No humans. No bodies.

The drizzle stopped and a frail wash of moonlight fell through the scrim of scudding clouds, illuminating their surroundings. What they'd taken for formless lumps in the darkness were actually the bodies of men and women strewn along the far edge of the clearing. Hold On spotted a red, meaty hunk placed on a stone with intricate carvings, and his eyes seemed to stumble in his head. Horror engulfed him.

"It's a heart! A human heart!" Hold On felt his legs buckling.

"Hold On!" Estrella screamed.

The stallion managed to recover and his legs stopped quivering. In the pale moonlight, the horses could all see the body from which the heart had been cut. And there were other bodies as well, also with gaping wounds.

"That's — that's . . . a shoe print. Centello," Angela said. "Centello has been here."

"And Grullo, and Arriero . . . and Bobtail." Corazón started naming the horses whose tracks she could identify. She walked slowly, still stiff-legged, and studied the hoofprints.

"But none of the dead are the Seeker's men," said Hold On.

"I don't understand," Estrella gasped. "Did the Seeker do this?"

"I don't know, but this is not the work of a Shadow Eater. This is the work of men." Hold On spoke in a voice he had never before used. "Men did this!"

The two mares seemed rooted to the ground. "No! No! The Seeker would never!" Angela insisted. "I heard about this on First Island. The Chitzen, they sacrifice their own to their gods."

"I heard it, too." Hold On shook his head. "But I never believed . . ." His voice dwindled as he looked down at the broken stones. There were stone heads and arms and legs of animals and men. These had been the Chitzen gods. The Seeker and his men must have smashed them.

Then a squeal pierced the air, a sound like nothing Estrella had ever heard, and she spooked. "That's not a horse!" she cried.

"It's a baby!" Hold On yelled as he wheeled about.

"A foal?" Sky asked.

"A human baby!" Hold On galloped down a path through a thin stand of trees, and the rest of the horses ran to catch up.

In the next clearing, a group of humans was gathered in front of a well, over which perched a rough-hewn carving of the Virgin. Not the Seeker's men, but men of the New Land. One man in a long white cloak, his hair clotted with blood, held a baby dangling over the well's dark mouth.

Hold On was confused. The white people's God was here. *But the Virgin does not take babies,* he thought. Then it became clear to him. The horses had stumbled onto a war of gods. The Seeker had attacked the new men's gods and now the men were frightened and trying to lure their gods back. They would give anything, even their babies.

The disgust Hold On felt that moment for humans rose like bile in his throat. He charged, and the man in white stumbled in alarm. A woman darted out and snatched the baby from the man's arms, then ran away sobbing. The crowd screamed and scattered, cowering in fear as the horses ripped through the throngs.

The five horses ran as if they were still in the thick of it. They could not run hard enough or fast enough to get away from the awful killing place. When they finally stopped, they were all sweating heavily. They had left the jungle behind and emerged onto a high flat plain, each full of the terror of the heart dripping blood on the stone and the baby held over the well.

"I don't understand. I just don't understand what was happening back there." Estrella was breathing heavily. It hurt to speak, but she had to know.

"It was the strange new men who did that," Angela said.

Hold On looked at her. What was she really trying to say?

"Yes, it was the new Chitzen," Corazón concurred.

"But did you see the prints of Centello, Arriero, and dear old Grullo?" Angela asked.

Estrella couldn't believe what she was hearing. She flinched and felt her withers tighten up, her shoulder muscles contract. Something made her nervous about the way the old mares were talking, and it was obviously disturbing Hold On as well.

"Angela, Corazón, listen to me," he said harshly. "It wasn't only the new Chitzen who murdered back there. It was Ibers as well. Men like the ones who curry you, who bring you water and grain. Who put bits in your mouth and saddles on your back!" Hold On was roaring now. "Men who call themselves masters. When they cannot master, they murder!"

Corazón and Angela were still for what seemed like a long time. There was a wildness in their eyes, as if they'd been spooked by something inside. They began to paw the ground, snorting and wheezing in renewed agitation. Angela curled her neck in tightly, tucked her muzzle close to her chest, and began to take small mincing steps in place. But she seemed unconscious of what she was doing. It was as if her mind had fled from her body. The motions were unthinking, automatic.

"She's doing the threshing step!" Hold On whispered to Estrella. Corazón began to make the same dainty steps. "Poor things," he murmured. His head drooped and he gave a mournful whinny.

"The mares." His voice seemed to break. "They . . . they are caught between two worlds — the Old Land and the New."

Then he turned to the mares. "Listen to me. Your masters are gone. You're not in a wheat field. There's no need to thresh. That work is over. You're free, Corazón. Free, Angela."

Angela stopped in place. "Angela?" she said in a soft whispery voice. Her large dark eyes swam with confusion at the sound of her own name. "I like my old name."

"Fea?" Hold On uttered in disbelief. "You liked being called Ugly?"

"And I liked mine, La Vieja — Old One," Corazón cut in.

Hold On shook his head. *They are hopeless. Even after what they have just seen, they are hopeless,* he thought.

"What are you, loco?" Estrella blurted in a loud snort.

"We want to find the others. Grullo, Arriero," Angela replied. "We're too old to learn these new ways and to forget the old." She glanced at Estrella. "They didn't treat us poorly, the Seeker and his men."

"They threw us off the ship!" Estrella said.

Corazón stepped forward. "But remember, the blacksmith said that we were strong and that we would make it to land and we did! We made it! They'll be happy to see us. And we will serve them well, as our sires and dams have and their sires and dams before us. It is in our life chain. It is in our blood."

Angela drew herself tall and once more arched her neck so her chin groove nearly vanished.

Hold On blinked. It was as if Angela had a bit in her mouth. Why did the two mares want to go back? What was there to go back for — combat, the burden of a fully armored soldier and his sharp spurs? A trip across an ocean in a sling? He did not know what exactly to do in this new land, but he sensed that the filly did. Perlina hadn't been simply a smart horse but, like so many pale horses, was said to have an "old eye" or "an eye of time." It was an eye that could see back to the ancient dawns when the horses first ran on this earth. They ran! Free in their own coats, their necks stretched out as they were meant to be. And these two mares wanted to go back to the Seeker! Age was no excuse. He was old, older than Angela and almost as old as Corazón, and yet he wanted to go on!

He turned to the mares. "You want to go back to the Seeker and to all that? To the Ibers and the Chitzen and all that blood?"

Both the mares' heads drooped. Angela nickered so softly, the others could hardly hear her.

"What did you say, Angela?" Hold On asked.

"I want a world with no Ibers and no Chitzen. Just . . . just . . . animals. I'd even prefer crocodiles and Shadow Eaters to the Ibers and the Chitzen!"

"So you'll stay with us?" Estrella asked.

Slowly, both Angela and Corazón nodded.

The horses moved on. The hoofprints of the Seeker's herd grew fainter and less frequent as the day waned. Estrella was waiting for darkness to fall. She needed to find the stars.

North. North. The only thought in Estrella's mind was north. It wasn't enough to have the scent of the sweet grass lingering in her head. Sometimes the scent was quite strong, but other times it faded until it was only an elusive taste on the wind. She needed the guiding star, the star that never moves. The words of her dam came back to her as clearly as if

Perlina were whispering in her ears. *You know when the groom comes and puts the water in our bucket how he takes that cup, a dipper? There's a star picture that looks like that, and the cup points directly toward the star that never moves. The men call it the North Star.*

Estrella knew now what she must do — find the water dipper in the sky. But first they must get far away from the men. They'd left the tangled world of the jungle, and when darkness came, she would look straight up into the sky and see the starscape, the million bits of light that cut the night. If she could just find the pointer stars in the cup that showed the trail to the North Star. She stumbled.

"What is it?" Hold On asked.

"When darkness comes, help me find the star picture of the water dipper."

"The water dipper?" Sky asked.

"We know the dipper," Hold On and Corazón both answered together.

"And so do I!" Angela said.

"It's grazing wisdom," Hold On said.

"What's that?" Sky asked. But Estrella felt she knew what Hold On meant. She remembered her dam telling her about the meadow.

"You see," Hold On said to the filly and the colt, "in the Old Land, we were taught things like gaits, and then there were things we learned out in the meadows where we grazed. These were the things that humans could never teach a horse. We learned about the changing shape of the moon, about the motion of the stars. Where the best clover grew. When our saddles had been taken off and our mouths freed of the bit — that was when we tasted the life we were meant for."

They did not have to wait long before the eastern sky darkened — "the sky we left behind," as Hold On called it. The first stars of the dipper lifted over the dark edge of the night. The horses stood with their tails to the wind as they watched the seven points in the star picture climb. They burned with a bright intensity.

So these, thought Estrella, *are the stars I was named for — these and a thousand other stars that will soon scatter through the night.* She felt a kinship with all of them and at the same time she sensed that the light was very old, very ancient, and had taken a long time to reach the earth on which they now stood.

Estrella knew that, old as the stars were, the last herd must have seen their same light as well. They were all star-bound, both the last herd and the first herd. Once again, the scent of the sweet grass streamed through the filly's mind and she felt her heart race. The stars at the end of the dipping cup pointed toward the blazing light of the North Star.

"We have it!" Hold On exclaimed quietly. "We know north for sure now."

The scent of sweet grass became stronger still in Estrella's mind. She saw Hold On peel back his lips and tip his muzzle up. *He's caught it! He's caught it! He smells the sweet grass, too!*

With Estrella in the lead, the five horses began trotting at a slow and steady pace north. As the dipping cup rose in the night, they followed the North Star, traveling farther inland from the coast. It was easier without the jungle to hold them back. The ground felt firmer beneath their feet and they could move more swiftly.

The countryside was very different. The dense green of the jungle had been swallowed up and the land stretched out before them, dusky and muted in the moonlight. In the distance, they could just make out the contours of low hills rising slowly against the darkening sky. The land seemed empty, a place of infinite solitude with only the sound of the wind and the occasional cry of a night bird rising in flight to disturb the peace.

When the moon was still high, they came to rest under the spreading limbs of a tree they had never before seen. There were no palm fronds to cast jagged shadows on the ground, but rather tiny, delicate leaves.

Angela turned to Corazón with delight in her eyes. "Corazón! It looks as if you are wearing the finest lace mantilla."

"What are you talking about?"

"The way the moonlight shines through the leaves has spread a lacy pattern on your back."

"Maybe it's a dress rather than a mantilla. No mistress of mine ever wore her mantilla on her back. Only her head."

Hold On snorted — *Dresses! Lace! Will these old mares ever learn to forget?*

Estrella could read Hold On's disdain but tried to be gentle with the older horses. "I've never seen lace or a mantilla, but I think you look very pretty, Corazón. I really do."

The nights were clear for several days as the horses followed the dipping cup and the North Star across the sky. They inscribed its path in their minds, so even when it rained and the stars were not shining, they knew the direction they must head.

Estrella had never forgotten that her dam was named for the color of the just before. She made a point never to fall asleep near the dawn, for that was the time when she felt Perlina's presence most strongly. One morning, after the stars had vanished and the sky was just growing light with the pale pink of the dawn, a silvery glitter streaked the sky. Caught by the light of the rising sun, the streak turned bloodred and glared on the horizon.

"It's a comet!" Hold On said, shaking himself awake. His ears flattened and he peeled back his lips and tipped his muzzle as if he were trying to smell something. Soon the other horses were awake and looking nervously at the horizon. An owl screeched and flew out from a tree, his white face caught in the reflection of the sun.

"It's a bad sign, isn't it? A vile star," Angela nickered. Estrella looked to Hold On. He flinched from his shoulders to his withers. Five horses stood trembling in the dawn light, mesmerized by the "vile star" that Hold On called a comet. No one moved and no one dared to speak.

Not far away in the City of the Gods, the Golden One, the chieftain of all chieftains, stood on a terrace on his palace in the middle of a lake, trembling in fear as he watched the comet. Two days before, lightning had struck the city's highest pyramid. Sacrifices had been made — so many that the gutters of the temple plaza spilled blood — and yet the gods were still angry.

"The gods never sleep," he muttered. And he, the most powerful emperor, could do nothing, absolutely nothing but receive all the dreadful reports from his scouts. His interpreters were busy trying to make sense of all the troubling signs. The first had been a startling dream the emperor had more than a month ago, a dream of a four-legged creature with feathers on its head and a neck like licks of flame. And was not this the year that the god who had deserted them promised to return?

But astride this creature was a strange man in a helmet. They were one, fused, man and beast together.

Now there was not just one of these peculiar man-creatures, but many to the south and east of the city, and they had told his messengers they wanted gold. They had pranced along a beach in a mighty display. They had odd machines that disgorged light and fire and stones into the air. It was said they had a disease that could be cured only by gold, and their leader had sent a helmet that was to be filled with gold. Dutifully, the Golden One had done so. But the god returned again with his fearsome man-creatures.

The Golden One did not know what to do. He had ordered the priest to cut out the hearts of countless people. The altars in the temples reeked of blood, and yet the new gods kept coming. Kept wanting more gold, more gold. Every day they drew closer. He had no choice but to open the gates to these gods and their lust for gold. A war between the gods would bring ruin. Not only to his city, but to the universe.

For several days, the horses watched the comet appear each evening, often toward the end of the night in the time of the just before. Would it never leave? It ruined the pearl gray of the skies. In Estrella's mind, it seemed to taint the memory of her dam and her lovely coat. The filly began to dread the dawn.

Infierno, Hold On thought one morning as they came to a crest. The red of the rising sun spilled across the valley below, like flames from hell. If they descended into this valley, that was what it would be — a hell through which they must pass. Hold On could see that there were human villages scattered throughout. They had to avoid them — there would be either Chitzen or Ibers, and the men would clash and blood would spill. The red streaks of the morning sun were simply a reminder that this quiet valley could turn to blood in an instant.

Still, Hold On believed they had no choice but to move forward. He could smell water in the valley, and the horses were desperately thirsty. Water had been scant the last two days.

The filly seemed nervous. She kept glancing toward the valley and then back to Hold On. All of them could sense that there was water in the valley, but the smell of men had them agitated.

"This way." Estrella jerked her head. "We'll go around the valley."

Hold On blinked. Were Estrella's large dark eyes, so like her dam's, a mirror for another eye deeper in her mind, that storied eye of the time some pale horses were said to possess?

The way around the valley was long and would take them off their course. But the horses followed Estrella, followed her even as the country grew more arid, the grass shorter, and the lace trees and their shade fewer and fewer. They came to the bed of what had once been a river but was now no more than a braided strand of foul, shallow water on beds of sand. The water gave them cramps deep in their bellies.

At times, the way became rocky. Occasionally the land dipped into steep gullies that they followed onto parched sections full of cracks. The sun blazed down during the day. It was hard to think of the water they might have missed by skirting the valley. But Estrella was sure the valley would have yielded blood as well as water. Up on the dry plain, they often saw tendrils of smoke rising from the valley, from villages that had been razed.

The horses' tongues hung out. Somewhere, they all lost the last of their shoes. Angela and Corazón did not seem to mourn. Their hooves quickly toughened and they felt a more direct connection with the ground and the subtle shifts in terrain and its textures.

Finally, a few days past the immense valley, they picked up the scent of fresh water and headed toward it. Soon they began to see forage — reedy grasses and stunted trees that nevertheless yielded sweet acorns and pine nuts. They came to a hillock and climbed it in hopes of spotting a pond or even a lake. Instead, they saw twin mountains in the distance, capped with snow.

"Meltwater!" said Corazón, and Angela and Hold On nickered in delight.

"Meltwater?" asked Sky. "What's that?"

"It trickles down from the mountaintops, especially white-capped ones like those. That's snow!" Corazón explained. The young ones had never seen snow.

Hold On was excited. "We can't be far from water now."

The horses kicked into a gallop and headed for the peaks.

After several hours, they spotted a streak of blue glinting across a vast swath of land.

"A lake!"

As they drew close to the lake, the wind shifted and an unmistakable scent assailed them.

"Centello!" Hold On snorted. "The stallion is near." *And so are the men!*

CHAPTER 9

We Are Gods Here!

"But water!" the colt said. "Water is near."

Hold On's and Estrella's gazes locked and they flattened their ears. Estrella felt her back legs tense, as if her body were telling her to bolt.

The odor of the great dark stallion with the blaze of a lightning bolt on his forehead was thick in the air. Estrella clamped her eyes shut and felt something turn deep in her gut. She remembered vividly the arrogant stallion eating grain from the Seeker's helmet. She recalled his disdainful glance at Perlina. Estrella's withers trembled. The stallion's presence made her anxious, but except for Hold On, none of the others seemed worried at all. They were too eager to get to the water.

Thirst had taken a toll on the two mares. Angela and Corazón were breathing heavily as they approached the lake. Just as they were about to step onto a narrow strip of beach, they heard Centello's familiar snort.

"Need water, do you? Don't drink that. It's no good."

"It smells fine to me," Estrella said.

"What do you know?" Centello gave Estrella the same disdainful look he'd cast so often at her dam.

A *lot*, Hold On wanted to say, but his throat was so parched he could hardly speak. He took in Centello's *recinto*, the small enclosure put up hastily by the Seeker and his men.

"It's *agua malo* — you'll founder if you drink it," Centello called. "Come round to the other side of the *recinto*. There's a full trough of good water."

Corazón, Angela, and Sky rushed over, but Estrella stood her ground. She was thirsty, too, but also fearful. Hold On, however, lowered his head and began to wave it from side to side aggressively. He was ready to attack, but attack what? Estrella tested the air and could find no trouble. Stiff-legged, she moved forward. She knew that Hold On was not following. But she was so thirsty.

Angela, Sky, and Corazón had pushed their muzzles through the *recinto* fence to drink, and Estrella nudged her way in to take a long draught of water. Soon she felt Hold On's comforting presence beside her. While they drank, Centello began to speak rapidly.

"This is it. This land is the dream come true! The Seeker's dream." Hold On paused mid-gulp to look up at the stallion. There was an odd, frantic quality to Centello's talk. He tossed his head, his eyes sliding about wildly.

Let him talk, thought Hold On. All Hold On wanted to do was drink and then get away as quickly as possible.

"You've never seen such a city in your life!" said Centello. "Temples gilded in gold. It makes the cathedrals of the Old Land look like peasant huts! And the chieftain of chieftains, he wears shoes with gold soles —"

"So?" Hold On cut in.

"'So'? What do you mean 'so'?" Centello asked.

"Why are you telling us?" Hold On asked. Estrella thought it was a good question. She kept her head down and continued to drink.

"Aren't you surprised to see us?" Sky asked. "We didn't drown. . . ." He hesitated. "Estrella's dam was killed by a shark. That was terrible."

"Oh, yes, I'm sure. How awful for you." Something in the stallion's tone made Estrella flinch.

Hold On slid his eyes toward the darker horse. *What's he up to?* Hold On wondered.

"You should stay," Centello said.

"Why?" Estrella asked. "What is there for us here?"

"Little one, you know nothing."

The stallion's arrogance made her bristle.

He turned his attention again to Hold On. "Listen to me, Gordo —"

"That's not his name anymore," Estrella snapped. "It's Hold On. Espero."

"Espero," Centello sneered. "Is that *espero* as in 'hope,' or 'wait'?"

"A little of both, I think," Hold On replied evenly, and lowered his head to drink again.

Centello poked his face through the gap, drawing in close to Hold On. "This land is where dreams come true. This is where we belong. This is better than the Old Land. You don't understand."

"What don't I understand, Centello?" There was an edge in Hold On's voice. A few other horses in the *recinto* had drawn closer. They were looking at the newly arrived horses as if they'd never expected to see them again.

"We are gods here!" said Centello. "The new men think we're as powerful as the Seeker."

The two mares were making gusty puffs in between their deep swallows of water, but Estrella could see they were listening.

"*¡Estúpido!*" Hold On replied with a low snort.

"Don't call me stupid!" Centello snapped. "Let me tell you something. There's a village back near the coast. The new men tried to attack our foot soldiers. Then the Seeker led the charge out from the trees where we had been hiding. We came galloping and the new men saw us for the first time. They were stunned! They'd never seen a horse before. And Alvaro — you know Alvaro? He rides Grullo, over there in the corner of the *recinto*."

A dun-colored stallion with high-set eyes and curved ears turned toward them but didn't come over to listen. *If he's a god,* Estrella thought, *he's an indifferent one.*

Still, Estrella was becoming increasingly nervous. She didn't like the way Centello's story was going or the way Angela and Corazón were looking at him with a kind of wistful longing. Even Sky seemed intrigued. "Well," continued Centello, "Alvaro somehow falls off Grullo, but by the Virgin if he does not jump right back on!"

"So?" said Hold On again.

"Don't you understand? They thought Alvaro and Grullo were one! That they were a god that could split apart and rejoin as it pleased. A god that could break in two and survive! They believe we are immortal. You should have seen them. I repeat: We are gods here!"

"Then tell me this, Centello." Hold On lifted his head high. "If you are gods, why are you and Grullo in the *recinto*, and the Seeker and Alvaro are not?"

Just then, like flying snakes, a flurry of lassos whipped through the air.

"*¡Perfecto!*" someone behind them yelled as loops settled on their necks.

Hold On shrieked and reared, but the loop had him firm. One loop caught Estrella and one caught Sky. Corazón was lassoed, too. The loop for Angela had missed her head entirely, yet she stood there docilely.

Estrella and Sky reared, but their front legs became hopelessly entangled and they collapsed onto the ground. Estrella kicked out wildly and tried to roll back on her feet. She'd never been on her back in her life. She was terrified, and Sky kicked Estrella as he writhed to right himself. Another loop landed on Estrella's hind leg and pulled tight. She tried to yank out of it, but her leg was caught fast, pulled taut behind her.

A cautioning hand came toward her muzzle and Estrella took a ferocious snap at it. She heard an Iber curse and someone punched her hard in her muzzle.

The scent of the sweet grass vanished and the stall walls on the ship loomed in her mind. She could almost feel the chafe of the sling. How could it all end so quickly? Perlina's dream — the scent of sweet grass, the scent of home, and the scent of freedom — all fraying now. The dream was dying.

Hold On was still on his feet, his powerful body pulling against the lasso that had him tight. His shrill screams were laced with curses, and his eyes had rolled back in his head until they appeared like two white moons glaring at the sky.

"Estrella!" came a cry, and the young groom raced out from the scrub with the blacksmith limping behind him. One of the Seeker's men walked over to Centello and stroked his muzzle, pressing some sweet to his mouth. "*¡Bueno! Bueno, amigo.*"

Hold On cut his eyes toward Centello and bellowed, "Some god who betrays his own!"

But Centello ignored him and lapped up the sugary treat.

The next moments were confusing to Estrella and Sky. Hold On continued to rear and shriek, but a quiet resignation seemed to envelop the mares, and they stood still as halters were fitted over their heads.

Estrella had felt a halter only when she had been lifted from the hold to be cast overboard. They had flung her away and now they were reeling her back into their world. The world of the bit, the saddle, and the rope. She whinnied shrilly as the halter descended.

"No! No!" she screamed. The smell of men was all around her, pulling her to her feet. Men and their sweat. Men and their rancid dreams. The masters were back. She was choking on the stink of it. Her eyes slid back in her head as the rope tightened around her neck.

The little groom stroked her. "Don't worry, little one," he said as he tried to fit the harness to her shaking head. "Everything will be all right. We'll lead you to a palace now. I prayed that you would make it. It is a sign of God."

Estrella had been gone so long from the language of the Iber men that it seemed unfamiliar and strange. She tossed her head again, but the groom tightened a strap connected to the halter and soon she could hardly move. The halter and strap had an odd smell, animal-like but slightly salty. Was it possible that it was made from the hide of some animal?

The idea unnerved Estrella, and she began heaving and panting, then tried to give a buck with bound legs. A whip lashed through the air and slapped down on her hindquarters. She screamed and reared, dragging the little groom up into the air. Another rope dropped around her neck.

"She's a wild one," someone yelled. "Twitch her, then hobble her hind foot! Like we did for Gordo."

Someone grabbed Estrella's upper lip and slipped something over her nose. She felt a cold hard thing pressing against her gums. She was so focused on her mouth and nose that she hardly noticed that someone had looped a strap on her hind leg. She hopped and almost fell. How was she to walk? Then it burst upon her — that was the point. She couldn't walk, could only make pathetic little hops. She felt a darkness begin to fill her. *They are breaking me. Breaking me!*

The men were grabbing, twisting, destroying her freedom, and with it came a feeling new to her — utter and complete humiliation. She thought of the fleeting figure of that tiny horse against the windswept sea of sweet grass and felt shamed and disgraced.

Something hardened within her. Let them punch her, whip her. Let them kill her, but they would not break her. No matter how many ropes they tied her with, no matter how many halters they put on her head, or bits they shoved into her mouth, she would never allow herself to feel this humiliation and shame again.

She and Hold On were the only ones to be hobbled. The twitch twisted their muzzles so they couldn't whinny. The only sound they could make was the most pitiful little windy squeak.

The men walked the horses until they came to a long causeway that cut across the vast lake. Ahead, looming in the growing darkness, was a massive mound that appeared to have steps carved into it. Other lesser structures melted out of the evening. Estrella had never seen anything like this. They were being led into a vast place — no mere village but a place where hundreds of villages had been brought together. The huge pyramid dominated everything.

Estrella could not turn her head, but she slid her eyes to the side and saw hundreds of Chitzen gathered to watch the procession of horses. Some fell to their knees.

"See how they bow to us, Gordo?" Centello called. Twenty Chitzen, some just children, bowed deeply and pressed their hands to their hearts, muttering softly in a language none of the horses had heard before. Centello nodded to them as if receiving their worship. "I have been in many battles, many wars," said Centello, "but this conquest was the easiest. And it was because of us! Horses. We won almost without fighting because they think we are gods."

Estrella flattened her ears. Did everyone think the horses were gods? Estrella and Hold On hobbled forward in the clumsy gait, their legs tied and their noses twisted up. Was this any way to treat a god? Estrella noticed that not all the Chitzen bowed. Some of them watched with eyes that betrayed a glimpse of skepticism, anger, or pain. Not all were worshipping.

Angela picked up her pace and lifted her head proudly, as if enjoying her new status as a god.

She thinks she's a god now. She really does, Hold On thought to himself. *Since when are gods hobbled like Estrella and me? Tell me that, foolish mare!*

"I can hardly believe it," Angela neighed softly as she strutted down the causeway, picking up her hooves high in a *paso alta.* "I feel as if I am in a dream!"

"This is a place of too many dreams and too many gods," Grullo muttered, breaking his long silence.

They came to the end of the causeway, to the base of the steps of what Centello said was the palace of the king, the Golden One. Near the base were several smaller structures, and from one came the distinct smell of animals — goats, pigs, and more horses.

Hold On grew even more agitated as a groom he recognized stepped forward with a saddle. The stallion whinnied shrilly and tried to rear on his hind legs, but it was impossible to hold his weight on only one leg. He collapsed in an enormous crash. Angela and Corazón gasped, and Estrella whipped her head around. *He's broken a leg!* she thought, horror shooting through her withers. But his leg was undamaged. He lashed out with it and managed to kick the groom, who shrieked in pain, dropped the saddle, and ran.

The Seeker stepped forward and shouted at Hold On. The war dogs from the ship — the huge mastiffs and the wolfhounds — surrounded their master. The Seeker drew out a long whip and cracked it in the air. The other horses froze, but Hold On rose up and hopped around on his three legs as the groom repeatedly made attempts to approach him with the saddle.

The Chitzen were enthralled. The gods were fighting! They had never seen such a display. The horses had never seen it, either. The bond between the horses and their grooms and riders had mostly been close.

It took three grooms and the blacksmith pitching in to subdue Hold On. They managed to get a second twist on the gray stallion's muzzle, and it brought him to his knees.

Estrella gasped. Hold On was utterly powerless now. He could do nothing as they put the saddle on him and fixed more ropes to his halter.

He's done, Estrella thought. She could tell by the dull light in his eyes. The old stallion had been brought down.

CHAPTER 10

When the Gods Be Mortal

There were seventeen horses in the newly constructed stables beneath the pyramid. Each horse had its own stall, and Hold On was placed next to Estrella. The grooms had left the saddle on him, and he'd stopped trying to shake it off. The old stallion had gone completely silent. His eyes were clamped shut and he was shivering hard.

"Why did they leave the saddle on you?" Estrella whinnied softly. Her restraints had been removed.

She hoped Hold On would answer. He had stood completely silent since they had put him in the stall.

After what seemed countless minutes, he answered, "To get me used to it. I'll pretend. What other choice do I have?"

"We've lost everything, haven't we?" Estrella said.

"Everything but our wits," Hold On replied. He was quiet for what seemed a long time. "Understand this, Estrella. We are safe only as long as we pretend."

The humiliation was creeping back. "Pretend we're not wild, not free? Pretend to like being caged and — and —"

"Enslaved?" Hold On said.

"How long do we have to pretend?" Estrella asked softly.

"I hope not long." He paused. "They are going to think they've broken me."

"But they haven't?"

"Wait and see."

Estrella sniffed and a drop of blood fell on the straw. "My muzzle is bleeding."

"That's good," Hold On said almost cheerfully.

Estrella sent him a sharp glance. "Good? What are you talking about?"

"I saw how some of the Chitzen looked at you as we crossed the causeway. There is not much blood on your muzzle, but they saw it. They were . . . how shall I put it? Surprised. And maybe relieved."

"Why?"

"Gods don't bleed," Hold On said quietly.

As the evening darkened into night, the old stallion seemed oblivious to his stall. In his mind, he was back on the beach where he had pounded down the hard sand, reliving the freedom of a back without a saddle, the feeling of his barrel chest free from a cinch. He marveled at the swiftness with which he had forgotten the gaits.

"*¡Hola!*" A cheery voice cut the night. The Seeker had come back into the stables and stood in front of Hold On's stall.

"He is calmer?" asked the Seeker.

"I think so," the young groom replied.

"Let's try him, then," the Seeker said.

Hold On flashed Estrella a look. He did not have to say a word. The light in his eyes said it all. *I am pretending. Be patient. Hold on.*

The stable was thick with tension as the little groom led Hold On from his stall. The stallion walked calmly toward the small plaza outside.

He is pretending, Estrella reminded herself. *Pretending.*

"Can you see what's happening?" Sky whispered from a few stalls down. Estrella craned her neck for a better view through the stable door.

"They're removing the hobble," Estrella said.

"What's he doing?" Angela asked.

"Just standing there."

"Oh, I hope he behaves himself," Angela sighed.

Behaves himself! The words enraged Estrella.

"What's he doing now?" Centello asked.

"Just . . . just sort of drooping his head." She felt her voice break. She had to keep reminding herself that Hold On was just pretending and that this was part of using his wits. "The Seeker is climbing onto a block."

"Mounting up," Grullo offered.

"You know," Angela began, "the royal infanta had a mounting block that was carved by one of the finest artists and inlaid with —"

"Oh, shut up!" Grullo said.

The Seeker swung one leg over the saddle horn. He gave Hold On a kick. But Hold On didn't move.

"What's happening?" Sky asked.

"Um — Hold On's not moving. The Seeker's kicking him hard. Wait! Now he's taking a step forward."

Hold On dragged himself languidly into a shambling trot. The Seeker dug spurs into Hold On's flank and thwacked him with the crop. Estrella spotted a trickle of blood on Hold On's soft flank. "I . . . I . . . don't know what's happening. I can't watch!" she said. Even though she knew this was part of a pretense, she couldn't bear to see it. Hold On's eyes had a dull glaze, as if a flame had been extinguished.

On the plaza, Hold On shambled in an odd gait. He could feel the Seeker unbalanced, gripping hard with his knees and trying to appear like the man-creature god they were supposed to be. Instead, the Seeker looked like a bobbling fool. Hold On was breathing heavily, wincing each time the Seeker dug in his spurs. Letting the Seeker ride him was part of Hold On's plan, but fear and shame were licking at him. The shame of the powerless. *Like them!* he thought as he glanced at the Chitzen looking on.

Hold On saw a small boy pointing at his flanks, where he

could feel a thin trickle of blood. *He sees I am bleeding! He sees I am no god.* This was the moment.

Hold On reared straight up and broke into a wild gallop. He stopped short, the Seeker lurching on his back, then reared again. He bucked, kicking out with his hind legs as violently as he could. The Seeker flew off his back and sprawled on the plaza. He couldn't move for several seconds, and when he staggered to his feet, blood streamed down his face from a deep gash in his forehead.

Hold On trotted around the plaza, his head held high and his eyes flashing. Had enough blood been spilled? Was this enough to convince the new men that the Seeker was no god? The Chitzen watching began to whisper and talk. Soldiers came out to break up the crowd.

Hold On galloped around the plaza wildly. A dozen grooms and soldiers rushed him, lashing out with whips. The ropes flew at him — ropes everywhere. On his head, slapped around his belly, his legs. And then he was down. Tied in the way they fastened a pig to carry him to the slaughter. The grooms quickly hobbled Hold On and they forced him, limping, back into the stable. "What did you do?" Centello yelled. "We heard yelling and, and — what did you do?"

"I threw the Seeker," said Hold On. "He is bleeding on the plaza."

"What?" Centello gasped.

"Why? Why would you do such a thing?" Angela screamed.

Hold On turned to her with a sly glint in his eye. "Because I'm a god?"

And now, thought Hold On, *we just have to wait.*

It did not happen quite the way Hold On thought it might. There was a sudden dank smell, the smell of the lake, and two shadows slipped into the stables. Hold On detected them immediately. They must have swum to the end of the causeway so as to sneak into the city unseen. This meant they were Chitzen and not Ibers, Hold On reasoned. The other horses smelled them as well, and stirred restlessly. The little groom was asleep and there were no other men about.

Looking out over the edge of her stall, Estrella saw the glint of a knife. The shadows sprinted to the nearest stall, Centello's stall. They slipped a rope over Centello's head and he began to rear, but one of the shadows gave a vicious lunge. There was an agonizing cry and then a gush of blood filled the stables with the familiar smell of metallic rot.

The horses shrieked wildly. The shadows clambered over the edge of the stall, a machete flashed, then flashed again, and soon the shadows were fleeing with the head of Centello between them. The dark stallion's eyes were locked in a terrible glare, as if he couldn't believe his own death.

Hold On reared in panic. The Ibers were the ones enslaving the Chitzen, stealing their gold and smashing their gods. Not the horses. He'd shown the new men that the horses were not gods, but the horses were not their enemies. "It's the Seeker!" he whinnied. "He's the one you're after! That is the god you want to kill." That was the god that Hold On had smashed. How had it gone so wrong?

Cries swelled from the city below, the roar of cheering new men. The young groom and the blacksmith gripped each other as they stood over the pool of blood by Centello's headless body. They were straining to make out the Chitzen's words, but they knew very little of the language. Then a light seemed to dawn in the smith's eyes.

"*Yo sé,*" he whispered hoarsely. "I know. The same for us. Quick! Release them. *¡Rápido, rápido!*"

Hold On blinked as the blacksmith approached to unstrap his halter. The young groom scrambled into Estrella's stall. The two worked fast and left the stall doors open when they were done. As they worked their way down the stable, one after another they swatted the horses on their rumps. "*¡Vaya! ¡Vaya!*"

Free! They are freeing us! Estrella thought as she tore out of the stall. Hold On was right by her side.

"Which way?" Sky yelled.

"Straight. Straight down the causeway!" Estrella whinnied.

The causeway was not far, but by the time the horses reached it, it was already slick with blood. Armed and screaming, Chitzen poured out of the thatched huts that lined the way. The clang of swords and the slash of daggers ripped the night. A rope spun through the air, its loop just missing Estrella's head. She veered left to dodge it and slammed into a man who was raising his machete as if to cut her down. Hold On reared and struck him with sharp hooves. The man's sword arm dangled loosely by his side and he collapsed, screeching in pain.

"This way! This way!" Hold On yelled.

The horses raced forward, but a knot of soldiers and Chitzen blocked their path. Behind them, crowds of men were fast approaching. *We're trapped!* Estrella thought frantically. She cried out as she saw soldiers with torches igniting something on the ground.

The water! It was their only chance. They had to make it to the edge of the causeway.

"To the water, follow me!" Estrella cried. But the horses were scattered. Sky skidded on the blood-slick paving stones. A man lifted up a huge cudgel to slam down on Sky's head. Estrella hurled herself into the man, knocking him sideways. "Get up, Sky! Follow me! To the water! Come on!" she screamed.

Angela raced forward.

"Where? Where?" The mare wheeled around.

"To the water! Get Corazón."

One of the war dogs tore through the throngs of people, his muzzle bloody. He caught sight of Estrella and charged. Hot rage rushed through Estrella. These were the dogs who had nipped at her as she swung above the deck on the ship. She wheeled and kicked and her hooves connected. She hated these dogs. The dog fell to the ground with a thud, his head bashed in on one side.

Then a great roar rose up behind her as a figure went flying from the very top of the palace. Two smears of gold streaked through the night. *It's the shoes!* Estrella thought. The shoes with the golden soles that Centello had told them about. The Chitzen emperor was falling from the top of the pyramid.

Just beside Estrella, a soldier screamed as one of the new men stabbed him in the stomach. An explosion flared out behind the horses. One of the light cannons had fired straight down the causeway. Flames tore the night, and a thatched roof burst into fire. An Iber soldier flung himself on Angela, trying to hang on and ride. But Angela bucked and the soldier went flying.

"Follow me, Angela! Follow me!" Estrella yelled.

The horses raced on toward the edge of the causeway, the lake glistening below. It would be a long jump into the water; Estrella paused. Angela quivered uncontrollably at the edge, her ears flat.

She'll never make the jump! Estrella backed up behind Angela and then charged, slamming into Angela's rump. The mare flew over the side of the causeway, screaming. With a massive leap, Corazón followed her. Hold On jumped next, and then Sky and Estrella flung themselves into the lake together.

When she surfaced, Estrella heard another splash behind her, and then another.

"This way!" she shouted. She swam as hard as she could. The lake was freshwater, so perhaps there were no sharks. She hoped there were no crocodiles. But she would have preferred both to what they were leaving. Estrella turned her head. Hold On was just behind her and Sky next to him, then came Angela and Corazón. But there were others from the stables as well. Behind them, up on the causeway, the new men were charging and the Seeker was in retreat!

"Swim!" she yelled to the other horses. "Swim!" There was a hissing sound as a rain of flaming arrows fell into the lake. "Duck! Swim toward the middle — they won't reach us there. Come on!" She circled back and began nipping Corazón and Angela on their hindquarters. "You can do it. Swim on." Her voice was soon ragged from urging, calling, beckoning, and screaming at the others. She would do anything to push the horses to swim on.

"Where are we going?" an unfamiliar voice called out.

"To the other shore and then north! Just follow me," Estrella answered. She tipped her head up and saw the dipper, and a deep thrill coursed through her. *Home. We are going home!* And once again, even through the smoke and blood, she caught the haunting scent of the sweet grass.

EARTH

CHAPTER 11

"We Are the First Herd!"

When the horses completed their swim across the lake of the City of the Gods, they clambered out on shore and began to gallop. They wanted to put as much distance between themselves and the city as possible. Finally, they drew up during the last shadows of the night under the spreading branches of a piñon tree and took stock. Five new horses had joined them.

A young filly, a blue roan, turned and asked, "Where are we going?"

Estrella cast a quick glance at Hold On.

"Away from men. We're seeking a new place," Hold On replied.

The filly looked at Estrella as if to say, *Why does he answer but you lead?* Estrella was grateful the roan didn't put her question into words. It would be hard to explain. Estrella, Angela, Corazón, Hold On, and Sky had become a herd. They'd been cast into the sea together, they'd traveled for many moons together. How could she explain what it meant to be a herd to these five new horses?

Hold On was thinking about more practical matters. The old stallion relished the sensation of his bare back, free from the burden of the saddle. It was doubtful the Seeker would track down the horses and recapture them, but there were still difficulties to face. With ten horses, there were bound to be. It was clear that the filly Azul, named for the blue tinge of her roan coat, was headstrong and young, but not as young as Estrella. How would she react to Estrella taking the lead? Hold On knew how the order of a group usually sorted itself out. Stallions protected the herd, but mares led. They had good heads for such things. They knew where the good grass grew; they knew which water holes in the meadows or pastures were the best. The blue roan might want to be boss mare.

Stallions were sensitive to danger. In the Old Land, this meant they kept a lookout for thieves who wanted to steal them. It was the stallion's job to warn the herd and to fight when necessary. Hold On felt he had been a complete failure when Centello had lured the herd to drink at the trough of the *recinto*. He should have known there was something sly going on. And though he was sorry that Centello had suffered such a gruesome death, he was furious at the stallion's deceit. But it was too late for anger now.

Hold On looked the new horses over. What would they be like? There were always troublemakers, but who would they be? Grullo, the dun stallion, was known to be reliable and steady. He never spooked. Hold On felt he could trust Grullo. But with the blue roan he was not so sure. Standing next to her was Bobtail, a bright bay stallion who was known for having a good mouth, so responsive to the bit that he turned quickly and smoothly. Now he was without a bit. Would he feel lost? Confused? There was a colt, Verdad, creamy white with black stockings. Would he be, like his name, truthful? And finally, there was the muleteer, Arriero.

The Seeker, some said, had favored Bobtail above Centello and lavished praise upon the stallion. Would he languish now without this praise? Hold On thought not. He was not as vain as Centello.

They had all lost their gaits quickly. When they had jumped into that muddy lake, it was as if all the paces and steps they learned had been washed away.

The horses traveled hard and fast over the next few days. The terrain smoothed out. The ground was firm and had few rocks on it, which allowed for speed. The horses took full advantage.

As they traveled, the territory changed around them, then changed again. They saw mountains in the distance, rising on a blue mist. They often passed through thinly forested regions with pine, pungent cedars, and broad-leafed trees — but none of the palmettos they had found near the coast. Unlike the jungle, where the mud sucked at their hooves, the way was solid here, their steps muffled by a carpet of fallen pine needles. The sunlight winked down through the boughs of the trees, casting spots of golden light on the ground. And then, like sparks igniting in the quiet forest, the horses began to see flutters of orange spiraling and twisting over them.

"Butterflies!" Corazón exclaimed.

They had seen butterflies in the jungle but never ones such as these. The wings of these creatures were bright orange with lovely black markings. As evening came, the butterflies began to gather in pendulous clusters that draped from the trees, folding their wings tightly shut. The orange vanished, and the butterflies looked as drab as dead leaves. No one would ever suspect the beauty they contained. Then, as the first drops of sunlight hit the trees, the butterflies erupted into a sudden conflagration. The entire forest flashed golden as the creatures opened their wings to collect the sun's rays. It was magical to the horses.

The best thing about the forests was that their canopies were not so thick as to obscure the sky. It was easy for Estrella to find the dipping stars. Soon she realized that, like the horses, the butterflies were also heading north. One morning, however, the butterfly magic ceased. The sky had clouded up and an insistent rain began to fall. The butterflies kept their wings clamped shut. The rain continued all day and into the night, and the air became colder. The butterflies started to quiver and those on the outside of clusters began dropping to the ground. Without the heat of the sun, they could not muster enough energy to fly. The horses had to leave the fragile creatures and hope that some would live and they might see them again.

After several days, the rain ceased and the horizon cleared. It had been too long since Estrella had seen the North Star. She hoped they were still heading in the right direction. Stepping out from under the shaggy shadows of the piñon tree, she lifted her head and scanned the sky for the North Star. It had just slipped over the edge of the horizon in the fading night and the rest of the dipper was following behind it, like a loyal herd.

Estrella swung her head in short arcs while flaring her nostrils and blowing. She could not help but wonder about the butterflies. Come morning with the first rays of the sun, she would look again for them — but the trees had thinned and there were few places for them to cluster.

There had been no scent of blood since the night of the horses' escape, but Estrella was always wary. For a moment she wondered if humans would go wild like horses if they left their huts, their villages, their way of life. Would they, too, forget what they were taught?

Just as she was wondering, Estrella caught, for the first time in days, the clear scent of the sweet grass. She shoved her ears forward, as if she might possibly hear the lush whisper of the wind through the sea of grass. The horses behind her went quiet and alert as they watched her. They knew she sensed something. The stallions, except for Hold On, tensed as if sensing a possible danger.

Hold On nickered softly. "There's nothing wrong. You'll soon enough understand. She . . . she knows."

"Knows?" the blue roan, Azul, asked. "How can she know anything? She's young. She's never been here before."

Hold On wheeled about and blinked at the blue roan. He almost thanked her for the insolent tone of her question, because suddenly Hold On knew exactly what it was about Estrella that made her their leader. He wanted to say, *But you see, Azul, that's precisely the point. She has been here before. Her bloodline goes back not just to the Iber Jennets or the Barbs or Arabians, but before.*

But how to explain this to the blue roan? To any of them? All their bloodlines went back, and yet Hold On imagined that Estrella's blood was like a sparkling thread glimmering through the filly's veins and illuminating their first origins, their first pastures, the first continent on which they had run and galloped.

Estrella was the youngest, but in a sense also the oldest. Hold On had seen things in that keen eye of hers. He sensed that what Estrella had was more like an instinct than a destiny. He had become more and more sure that Estrella had seen some sort of ghost horse from an ancient time that guided her as surely as the dipper. Hold On gave the blue roan a quelling look, but said nothing.

The black of the night thinned to gray, and the gray faded into the silvery dust of the just before. Estrella nickered to the others, "This way."

When the dawn finally broke, the clouds were so high that it was as if the bowl of the sky were filled with a luminous pink glow. The horses quickly fell into order. Estrella took the lead with Hold On just behind her on one side and Grullo on the other. The two stallions, Arriero and Bobtail, took the outer flanks. In the middle came Angela, Corazón, Azul, Sky, and the colt Verdad. Verdad and Sky nickered to each other.

"You have one blue eye and one good eye," Verdad said to Sky.

"They're both good. I can see from them both."

"You can really see from the blue one?"

"Yes."

"You know what they call a horse with a blue eye?"

"*Caballo con un ojo azul*, 'a horse with a blue eye,' I suppose," Sky answered.

"No," nickered Verdad. "They call a horse like you a glass-eye horse."

Sky snorted. "That's stupid. Do you think my eye will shatter?"

"I don't know. But that's what the Seeker and his men call horses like you — glass eyes."

"They don't know horses." Sky paused. "Not the way she knows horses." He nodded toward Estrella.

"The filly?"

Sky nodded.

"But why does everyone follow her? She is the youngest of us all. She didn't even touch land until she got to this country. She was born on the ship."

"She knows land now," Sky replied.

Verdad glanced nervously at Azul. "So does the blue roan. They say blue roans, you know . . ." His thought seemed to dwindle.

"What do they say? Is it like what they say about horses with one blue eye — glass eyes?"

"Well, our masters," Verdad began again. "I heard them say that blue roans are uncommonly intelligent. That they have all the colors, like a rainbow has all the colors and —"

Sky broke in. "Horses are not rainbows and the Seeker is not here! There are no masters here. Only horses that can lead, and others like Grullo and Hold On and the other stallions that protect us."

Verdad glanced at Azul as if expecting the filly to answer for him.

"What is it, Verdad?" Azul asked.

"Nothing," Verdad replied.

"It must be something. You looked troubled. I told you before, when you have troubles, you share them with me."

Why? Sky thought. It seemed odd. Why couldn't Verdad decide who he shared his troubles with? Azul wasn't his dam or his sister. Sky trotted up closer to Hold On.

Now Estrella looked up. There had been no moon when they fled the City of the Gods. Then it had swelled as they headed north, only to fade again to nothing. But she could see behind the scudding clouds a sliver thin as an eyelash. It had been a full cycle. *The land in this New World,* she thought, *is made for galloping.* The horses had pounded north, covering huge distances. In the jungle, they had made a fraction of the distance they now covered in a single day. Since their escape, they had passed through high plains, scrublands with shrunken trees and nary a blade of grass, then the forests where they encountered the magical butterflies. They had seen rolling hills that tumbled with low dusty grasses, and traveled for days on end through lowlands that grew with what the horses called sharp grass. The edges of the grass were jagged, and when the wind blew through it, there was a great whining sound.

Now the country seemed to lift itself out of the basin of these lowlands. There was a welcome quiet as the sharp grass receded and the wind buzz was swallowed into the vastness of the arching sky. The land became drier and drier, and as it did, the scent of the sweet grass seemed to recede.

Estrella sensed that some of the herd were doubting her. She almost could smell the dissension. Not from Hold On 'or Sky, but from Azul and possibly Bobtail as well. The two old mares were always gentle, but there was something in Angela's and Corazón's manner that seemed more faltering and hesitant than usual. Verdad was close to Azul, so easily influenced. Grullo and Arriero were still unfamiliar with Estrella. They seemed stalwart sorts and they were deeply respectful of Hold On. But were they strong enough to hold the herd together despite the burgeoning tension?

Sometimes the land was broken, as if old creeks or rivers had torn up the terrain. There were dust storms that would sweep across the broad plain, their outlier whirlwinds like twisting phantoms from another world. And on occasion, dramatic thunderheads stampeded across the sky. The air swelled suddenly with moisture, the clouds roared and split, and the rain lashed down, drenching the herd.

"The bones of the sky are cracking," Grullo would mutter. And indeed the lightning splintered like skeletons slamming against the night. At times like these, the horses would hunker down under the sandstone rimrock that was exactly the color of Estrella's coat — "with fewer burrs," they joked. The horses often stood face-to-face, grooming one another by running their teeth and lips down the withers and neck of whoever was closest. It was very soothing during the storms.

Once, Hold On was grooming Estrella and Estrella sensed that she should turn to Verdad, whom Azul had been grooming. At first, Azul gave her a sharp look, but just then, Sky showed up with a coat and mane full of burrs. "It was that last patch we went through before the storm. Those stick burrs were too high for me."

"Or just perfect for your withers," Azul snorted.

Estrella wondered why they hadn't done more grooming when they had first landed and were traveling through the jungle. It was so calming. She recalled her dam grooming her in the dim light of the hold. But that was in the slings; every time her mother tried to comb through Estrella's withers, Estrella's sling would swing away. It became quite frustrating for both of them.

This was entirely different. The earth never moved, not even when the air was quaking with thunder and the sky flashed against the night.

After the thunderstorms, the world would appear rinsed and fresh, ready for them, this first herd.

One morning, as the thin haze of the previous night's moisture cleared, strange, steep rock formations with flat tops appeared in the distance.

"Like my master's table," said Angela when they spied the first one.

"Were you accustomed to eating at your master's table?" Azul said with a snide look at the old mare.

"As a matter of fact, he brought one of those tables into the stables. It was Saint Eligius Day, and it was raining hard, so the blessing was said inside the stables. We were led forward one by one and given an apple."

"Who's Saint Eligius?" the blue roan asked.

"The saint for horses," Angela replied.

"My goodness," Corazón said, her voice rather dim. "I almost forgot him."

"He was an Iber saint," Hold On snapped.

"But he was the saint for horses, too," Angela insisted.

"What are saints supposed to do?" Estrella asked.

"To protect us, look out for us," Angela nickered almost dreamily.

Estrella snorted. Where was the saint on the day her dam died? "I don't think he did a very good job," Estrella said, thinking of her dam and Centello's severed head.

"Will there be saints in the New Land?" Sky asked.

"I hope not," Hold On replied, and tossed his mane as if he were trying to rid himself not only of the fly that had landed on his forelock, but every pesky thing from the Old Land.

The next day, there was a strange occurrence in the sky. On either side of the morning sun, there was a bright glow, as if two other, smaller suns had risen to make a halo surrounding the first sun.

"Sun ponies!" Hold On said. "I only saw them once before, in a meadow."

"Is that meadow wisdom?" Estrella asked.

"I suppose so. An old mare said they were supposed to bring good luck."

"Do you believe it?" Estrella asked.

"Not really. That's just superstition."

They continued on through the rough and broken country. The stallions, who rode as outriders, suddenly became alert, their ears twitching. The wind shifted and then the herd caught the scent. *Meat eater! Big meat eater!*

"Where is it?" nickered Estrella.

"I can't see it yet," Arriero answered. "Pack close!" Hold On, Grullo, and Bobtail took up defensive positions.

Some luck those sun ponies brought! Estrella thought.

"There it is!" Grullo whinnied. "And a mate!" The horses swung their heads.

Two immense catlike creatures were stalking down from the low bluffs. Their coats were unspotted, but otherwise they looked much like the Shadow Eater from the jungle.

Grullo and Bobtail pressed the southern flank of the herd, turning the horses and urging them to speed. The cats were the exact tawny color of the bluffs from which they had descended. They loped onto the flats at a leisurely pace and began to position themselves on either side of the herd.

They're waiting for us to tire, Estrella thought. The male was big — bigger than the Shadow Eater. Estrella's first instinct was to gallop, but she knew she had to slow her pace. The cats would wait until the horses had run themselves out and then they would split the herd and pick out the slowest or the most defenseless. It came to Estrella like a picture, a nightmare she had seen before. She whinnied the signal to slow.

"¿Lento?" Azul asked incredulously.

Hold On nipped her buttocks as a clear reprimand. *Don't question the boss mare.* Estrella saw this from the corner of her eye and it shocked her. She was the boss mare. She knew she was leading the herd north, but she was still so young. She wouldn't even be a full-fledged mare for a long time. Still, there was business to do. Boss, leader, jefe. The word didn't matter. She must act.

The herd slowed from a flat-out gallop to an easy canter. Estrella noticed that the cat on Hold On's side blinked and backed off a bit.

She whinnied, "What's the other one doing, Grullo?"

"The female, she's . . . uh, slowing, but she has her eye on Verdad."

They continued on at a lope for several minutes. Estrella hoped the cats would get bored, but the big creatures stayed behind them. The male peeled off to find a better attack position, but the female stayed where she was.

Estrella whinnied to Arriero and Hold On. "Steady now!

I'm turning the herd toward the cat. When I squeal, I want the stallions to break for her."

Hold On nickered in surprise. "You want us to fight?"

"Exactly!"

Estrella pivoted and the herd turned, no longer running parallel to the female cat but heading straight at her. Estrella whinnied the high-pitched command and the four stallions tore out from the herd and reared, their hooves striking at the flawless blue sky.

The female cat shrieked in surprise. One of Arriero's hooves struck the side of her head and she was stunned. Her mate flashed to her side.

This is bad! Estrella thought. Then, all at once, the four stallions wheeled around and leapt in place, making an enormous twisting monster in the air. The cats seemed to freeze at the spectacle.

The stalllions landed, and Arriero, the largest and most powerful, spun around and bucked. He caught the male with his hind hooves and flung him into the air. Blood spurted from the pale fur of the male's belly. His mate squealed and bolted.

The stallions were breathing hard, their deep chests heaving from the adrenaline that charged through them. Estrella raced up to them, and the rest of the herd followed. They approached the cat cautiously.

He was obviously dying. His mouth pulled back in a grimace to reveal two long fangs that could have easily torn any horse apart. He was gasping and grunting, and to Estrella's mind, he seemed to be saying, *Who are you? What are you?* It dawned on her that the cat had never seen their likes before. They were new creatures in a new world.

The cat's breath stuttered and his flailing slowed. He was barely moving now, struggling for each breath. He was noble and brave. He had not hung back in the middle of battle, and he had sprung into danger to help his mate.

Estrella bent her head low toward the cat and whispered the answer to the question he seemed to be asking.

"We are horses. We are the first herd!"

CHAPTER 12

Rumps to the Wind

The herd traveled on, rested, and then traveled once more. Estrella was spurred forward by the scent of the sweet grass and the image of the tiny horse. They had crossed so much territory now, and she didn't know how much more was ahead of them. The thought was daunting. But there were no more encounters with big mountain cats. They did, however, come across other animals they'd never seen before and who had never seen them. They'd pause at a respectful distance to observe each new creature they encountered.

Soon they learned to follow the droppings of sheeplike animals with enormous horns, for their trail often led to good grazing. It wasn't quite the sweet grass scent that lingered in Estrella's mind, but it was good grazing nonetheless. Once as they were foraging, a storm of orange butterflies rose in the bright morning light.

Estrella gasped. "It's them. They're back!" She walked closer to a milkweed plant, where three butterflies were resting. She noticed minuscule white beads on the milkweed. Instinctively, she sensed that these had been made by the butterflies.

"These white dots — the butterflies did this, didn't they?" she asked Hold On.

"I believe so," Hold On replied. "I've seen this sort of little dot in the Old Land. They are laying their eggs, I believe." He nodded at Estrella. "Smart filly you are!"

Estrella was pleased with the compliment. Hold On rarely praised. He was not an effusive animal. "Do you think I am, uh, how did you say it? Gaining meadow wis —"

Hold On's ears pricked forward and he shuddered. Butterflies would not cause a shudder like that, Estrella knew.

"What is it?" she aked.

The wind had just shifted and soon a scent enveloped them that answered her question.

"Deer!" said Hold On.

"Where there are deer, there are often men." He was trembling. "Men hunt deer."

"But, Hold On," said Angela, her dark eyes puzzled, "men don't hunt horses!"

Hold On cut his head sharply toward the mare. "No, Angela, they capture us!"

The horses detected no smell of men, nor did they smell big cats or other hunters. Still, they were nervous as they came across the deer. There were only three of the creatures, and

Estrella thought they were lovely. Small and delicate, they moved with an expressible grace and daintiness. They were curious, but hardly aggressive. And they were so quiet. The little one, smaller even than a newborn foal, was the most curious of all. He took a few tottering steps toward Sky and Verdad, who were grazing side by side, and nickered softly.

The herd was shocked. The older horses had seen deer in the Old Land, but these were different. They were slightly smaller and intensely curious. The deer had never seen a horse before, but when the fawn spoke, the horses understood. His tone wasn't too different from how deer spoke in the Old Land. All cloven creatures spoke somewhat alike.

"Are you my brothers . . . my big brothers?" asked the little fawn.

The sound of the fawn's voice was in a different range, more nasal than the speech of horses. "I — I don't think so," Sky replied.

"Your voice sounds funny!" said the fawn. "Is it because you're so big?"

"So does yours!" Sky replied. "Is it because you're so small?"

At this, the grown-up horses and the deer all made hiccuppy laughing sounds.

"Who are you? Big deer?" the fawn asked.

"We're horses come from far away," Verdad replied.

"We have never seen creatures so like ourselves, but then

again not quite." He tipped his head to one side as if he were contemplating the strangeness of it all.

Sky came closer, stretched out his neck, and blew softly. The little fawn stepped back and the doe laughed.

"We do the same when we encounter something new. What are you?" asked the doe.

"I'm a colt," Sky said.

"A colt. Our young'uns are fawns," the doe said.

"Are you a glass-eye like Sky?" Verdad asked, peering at the fawn's milky blue eyes.

"No, I'm blind," the fawn said. "But watch me! I can do everything any fawn can do!" He began prancing about, then bucked out his slender back legs. "And I can balance on my hind legs and hop a bit." The fawn continued to dance around, showing off his steps. He was as light as the balls of fluff from the cottonwood trees. Estrella noticed that the deer's hooves were split, which seemed to give them, or at least this little dancing fawn, amazing balance and agility.

"It's why he's so curious, I think," the doe answered. "He wants to know everything he cannot see in this world. And he's a fast learner." She nuzzled him.

The stag with his towering rack of antlers dipped his head regally to Estrella. "We welcome you. You are not meat eaters but grazers. There is plenty of bunch grass, and then beyond, there is the sharp grass and the buffalo grass." The stag went on for a bit about the various grasses.

"Is there one called the sweet grass?" Estrella asked.

"Sweet grass . . ." He cocked his head. "Yes, I believe I have heard of it, but it's far to the north. A long distance from here. But this grass is very good. Perhaps not quite as tender as the buffalo grass or the blue grama grass —"

The fawn, however, had grown bored and he interrupted.

"Perhaps you are like the Once Upons!"

"The Once Upons?" Estrella asked.

The doe turned to Estrella. "I can't explain the Once Upons. They are . . . a mystery. They were not deer or horses. They only had two legs, not four."

Estrella felt a chill run through her. Was the doe speaking of men?

"They're not here anymore?" Hold On asked nervously.

"No, not for a long, long time."

"Where did they go?" asked Grullo.

"No one knows. That's the mystery. They moved on, dissolved like dewdrops in the morning sun," the doe replied.

"But they left their pictures," the fawn said. He had grown quite excited and was almost dancing on his tiny hooves. "They did! I can't see them, but my ma tells me about them. And the ones cut into the rock I can trace with my tongue."

Estrella was not sure what exactly the fawn meant by "pictures," but she imagined it might be like the star pictures her mother had told her about. Or perhaps they were like the carvings of the Virgin.

The horses grazed with the deer family for the long sunny hours of the morning. Estrella stayed close to the doe and the stag. She was learning things from them. They had a curious way of marking territory by rubbing their heads against trees. They also told the horses that the mountain cats were not the only meat eaters. There were wolves as well, not as large, but with very sharp teeth.

"Ah, wolves!" Hold On said. "Yes, they were a danger in the Old Land, too."

"And then there are smaller ones. Very sly and with sharp teeth as well — coyotes."

"¡Perros zorros!" Hold On exclaimed. "We had those. They raided the chicken houses."

"Raspadores de hueso — bone scrapers! That's what we called them," Grullo said. "Cowardly brutes who'd come in after a larger animal made a kill, to pick out the eyes and any last flesh left on the bone."

Estrella listened carefully and could not help but wonder if she were gathering meadow wisdom. Each day, each night, they discovered something different and new. To think that in the beginning of her life, she had been confined to the tight, shadowy space of the hold. It seemed unimaginable now. She looked up and saw the ghost of the moon riding in the noon sky. It was like a shadow of what had been and what might come.

The country was empty, but beautiful. In the morning, when the sun was still under the clouds, the world turned a fragile and luminous pink. It was a land that had been sculpted by wind. There was fallen timber on the ground, weathered and carved by wind so it looked swirled like water, like the eddies of a lively stream. The wind was a force that could change the very substance of things. The long silvery grass could suddenly become a roiling ocean. Clouds stretched into sharkish shapes and fled before sudden breezes. It was a land of many changes, quick changes.

Indeed, as the horses drove farther north, they learned the weather could shift in a matter of seconds.

On one day not long after they left the deer, the sky began to darken as the herd grazed in the early morning. Dusky clouds rolled up on the horizon and there was a bite to the air. The older horses became fidgety and flinched from their withers to their rumps. Although there were no flies around, they swished their tails nervously.

Estrella turned her head to look at Hold On. His normally soft brown eyes seemed to shudder with light.

"What is it?" Estrella asked.

"Weather," Hold On replied.

"More rain?"

"Not just rain. Snow. The great whiteness."

Estrella pricked her ears forward. "It came to your pasture once?"

"It smothered my newborn colt."

Not drowned. But smothered. It was unimaginable to Estrella. Was the great whiteness like the shark? A huge sliding white shadow and then blood — lots of blood.

But when the snow came, it wasn't like that at all. First, there was a coldness that seemed to stiffen the air around them. The sky thickened to a color that was neither white nor blue but a metallic gray that reminded Estrella of the bit and the chains that the grooms shoved into her mouth. A wind started to howl that drove the cold straight into them, robbing their bodies of warmth. And then came an engulfing whiteness. Soon, they were all shivering.

The older horses — Grullo, Hold On, Bobtail, Angela, Corazón, and especially Arriero, knew what to do. They huddled up in the lee of an immense boulder in a rough half circle, with their rumps to the wind. The blizzard roiled across the broken land toward them. Puffs of sagebrush hock-high were soon swallowed up by the snow, leaving only the faintest lumps to show where they grew.

When the storm struck, the horses had wandered into a sink basin, perhaps an ancient lake that had dried thousands of years before. Now the basin was filling up with snow. The herd huddled closer together. The older horses began to reminisce about the times the whiteness had come to the Old Land. Hold On alone remained silent.

"This is not so bad," Corazón said. "I've been through worse, I think."

"The storms on the ship were worse than this," Angela added.

"Certainly!" Corazón replied emphatically. "I'd rather feel the weather and face it than be in that awful hold hearing the wind shriek and having the ship toss."

"But you're not facing it," said Grullo. "Our rumps are facing it."

"And you, Grullo," said Angela, "have the biggest rump of all."

They all snorted heartily at this. Their breath created a warm cloud of fog that hung over them. Despite the howls of the wind and the bitter blasting swirls of snow, there was something very snug and peaceful about the circle they formed.

The horses talked and told stories as the blizzard blew, long into the night. It was odd to Estrella that stories should bond them more than even the fight against the mountain cats. *This,* Estrella often thought much later, *is when all ten of us truly became a herd.*

When the blizzard finally ceased and the horses turned

their heads back to the world, the landscape had been trans-formed. They looked out on a crystalline world of white. In some places, there were snowbanks as tall as they were. But as deep as the snow was, it was light as down. They began to move out from the rimrock, and as they plowed forward, they sent up puffy explosions. Soon they were all frolicking, bucking and leaping, dipping their heads into snowy banks, then tossing up soft geysers of snow. The younger ones stuck out their tongues, enjoying the light tickles of the gently falling flakes. Sometimes they would munch up a mouthful, trying to figure out the exact taste of the fluffy whiteness.

"Look at this!" Sky exclaimed. The colt had lain down on his side, then carefully raised himself up again, leaving a nearly perfect impression of his body. Soon the others were trying the same thing. Estrella just tried resting her head on the side of a snowbank. When she backed away, there was a white silhou-ette of her profile with even the strands of her mane flowing as if she were running. But most fun of all was to run through the soft billowing undulations of the snowy masses. It was like a white sea — a sharkless sea.

If moving through water was called swimming, Estrella thought, what was cantering through snow called? She won-dered sometimes why she had so many questions. Did horses in the Old Land question as much as she did? The land that opened before her also opened her mind in ways that continually surprised her. She thought about the deer family. Had they made it through the blizzard? Would they have turned their rumps to the wind? They were so fragile — would they be smothered like Hold On's foal?

CHAPTER 13

Snow and Silence

The blizzard had come down on the deer family with no warning. There were no looming dark clouds on the horizon. They were out in open country a fair distance from rock shelter when suddenly the world turned white with snow and lashing winds. The deer were so light, particularly the fawn, that it was impossible to make real headway against the wind. For a time they moved downwind. The snow began to pile up quickly and the fawn, though nimble, had a hard time keeping up. The fawn had been born in the early spring and had never known winter. This was a late-spring storm, often the most severe type of storm in this part of the country. Although his parents found the impenetrable whiteness daunting, for the blind fawn, it was not that different from his normal world, except for the cold and the wind.

But as the snow kept driving down, the danger of the storm revealed itself. The deep snow muffled scent, and the fawn depended on his powerful sense of smell. If he could not smell, it was another kind of blindness. His parents slowed their pace and turned around often to scent mark so he could follow. But as the snow became thicker, the scent marks were covered up more quickly. Soon the fawn could smell nothing. Nor could he hear his parents' frantic calls over the roar of the wind. He bleated helplessly into the snarling gusts, but his calls were greeted by the growl of the wind. It felt as if the world as he knew it, his parents, the softness of his mother's belly when he nuzzled her while nursing, had been swallowed and he was alone. Completely alone.

He wandered aimlessly in the featureless land, cold and hungry, sometimes up to his neck in drifts. When he thought he was so tired that he couldn't take another step, he sensed a break in the wind. Like a yawn in the night, something hollow loomed ahead. He forced himself on and soon found a small, shallow cave. It was thick with snow, but at least it offered refuge from the wind. The fawn entered and burrowed down into the soft and deadly snow, with only his nose poking out to breathe.

It was the first time in his short life that he had not had milk before going to sleep. That he had not had a story told by the stag, that he could not feel the starlight or the moon rising as his mother described it to him. If the fawn had not been blind, he would have seen that high on the cave wall were pictures. Some were animals, but one was a carving in the rock of a Once Upon — a two-leg with a hump on his back and a long piece of wood in his mouth, through which he was blowing a tune. The picture was directly above the little fawn's head and it almost looked as if the figure was fluting him a lullaby.

When the wind outside the cave ceased howling and the storm ended, the fawn woke up. The cave had been a fine place to sleep. He was hungry, but most of all he was starving for his mother and father. He bleated loudly, hoping that they might be just outside the cave or perhaps in another cave nearby. But he heard no answering call.

The fawn took a cautious step outside. He walked a short distance in the deep snow, bleating. Suddenly, a strong scent washed over him. It was not his mother nor his father. It was a mountain cat.

The fawn frantically tilted his head one way, then another. His hearing was extraordinarily keen and he could hear the breathing and the even heartbeat of the big cat. Closer and closer the cat came. The fawn was so frightened that he stood in place, too scared to move. If he had only stayed in the cave, he thought. He had felt something in the cave protecting him, a guardian who hovered over him in his sleep. But there was no one to guard him now.

When it happened, it was quick. Quick and oddly silent. The fawn didn't make a sound. He felt a sudden, crushing weight and then he was dead. His filmed blue eyes stared up into the sky he had never seen. A short distance away, another creature lurked, waiting his turn, waiting until the cat had eaten its fill. Then the coyote would come in for the bits the cat had left, come in to scrape the bones.

Several days later, the horses came across a sheer wall of stone and paused to look at the strange markings on it. Estrella stood close and blew through her nose, then inhaled with her mouth clamped tight, making a sound that horses sometimes used to greet each other. "You're talking to a rock?" Azul sneered.

Estrella didn't answer. She was wrapped up in the images streaming across the rock face. Images of animals — of deer, of spiders, of wolves — and images of two-legs. Men! But not like men today. Men from the long ago.

These are the rock pictures of the Once Upons! Without thinking, Estrella stuck out her tongue and began to lick an image, tracing it as the fawn said he had done. She shut her eyes. The fawn was an uncommonly bright little creature, and though he was blind, she felt he saw more with his filmed eyes than most creatures did with their eyes clear.

She began to wonder again about the Once Upons. The doe had said they were a mystery, unexplainable. They had two legs. So that meant they were human. She did not like humans.

But if they had lived here so long ago, could they have ever been here at the time of the little horse? She thought not. For the little horse was very ancient. But had they lived at a time before the Ibers, before the Chitzen? Were the Once Upons the original two-legs, the original humans? And was there something she must learn from them and their time on this earth, something that she was meant to know even if she could never exactly understand it?

The other horses came in closer to look at the pictures.

"Look! Some are two-legs," Hold On said.

"The Once Upons," Estrella whispered. She was unsure who these Once Upons were, but something about them seemed different from the Ibers or the Chitzen. They were older, for one. And wilder. They'd lived so long ago, maybe in the time of the tiny horse she saw so clearly in her mind's eye.

Estrella walked along the wall, examining all the pictures carefully. And then she spotted it, a tiny, horselike creature sprinting across the rock face. The rock looked almost like a windswept plain, its fissures and striations the blowing grass. Estrella could almost smell the sweet grass. They were on the right track! She was sure of it. This little streaking figure was exactly the image she had seen reflected in Perlina's eye as the mare was dying.

The horses walked on under the shade of the rimrock. Estrella found three other carved figures of the tiny horse. Each time, she felt a sense of a new energy and a deeper connection to her dam and the flash in the dam's eye. In the jumbled land-scape of half-lost memory, the tiny horse was becoming a constant nearly as steady as the star that never moved. Until now, the search for the sweet grass and the blowing landscapes of the north had been only an instinct, a vague sense of a new way of life. But the quest was becoming more defined. Estrella knew that her journey was long from over, but the image of the tiny horse was in much sharper focus now. The herd was not simply on a quest, they were reliving a story, an ancient narrative that linked horses everywhere to that very first horse — the tiny horse that seemed to glimmer on the edge of dawn.

The day had grown very warm. Hold On said that he thought it was late spring and that the blizzard they had encountered had been the last blow of winter. The horses knew they were much farther north now. Hold On guessed that they were more than six hundred leagues from the beach where they had landed.

The shadow of a coyote slid across the rock face. They'd seen several coyotes since they'd arrived on the high plains of this desertlike country. Estrella found something unnerving about the coyotes. Their pelts were yellowish gray and they had long, sharp teeth that seemed too large for their small heads. For some reason, coyotes, although much smaller than the mountain lions, seemed scarier to the horses. Perhaps it was because of their stealth and the fact that they were often scavengers. The herd had the sense that the coyotes were always watching, waiting for an old horse to go lame, or a mare to lie down in a distant part of a meadow to foal. Then they'd sneak in and snap the tendon of a lame foot or run off with a newborn foal. Coyotes could slip through the narrowest cracks in a rock wall, and also thread through the shadows of the horses' minds, brewing nightmares.

Hold On told Estrella that in the Old Land, horses called coyotes *fox dogs* or *perros zorros*. For they were sly like foxes but fought like mad dogs. Unlike the mountain cats, they seemed to be able to hide in the smallest cracks and crevices. And then suddenly their slinking silhouettes would appear against the sandstone walls. The herd tried to ignore the coyotes as best they could. But each of the horses wondered how many coyotes were lurking in the cracks of the sandstone cliffs they passed. There could be a whole pack of them, and as a pack they would be terrifying.

The snow had melted away almost as quickly as it came, and the day grew warmer. The herd was walking at a leisurely pace, trying to keep out of the sun. Water seemed scarce in these parts, and the horses didn't want to work up a deep thirst.

They kept their eye out for coyotes as they traveled. Sky

spotted one on a cliff above them, his tail lifted high in the breeze as he peered down on the herd. Estrella noticed that the fur of his muzzle appeared darker, stained. She realized the stain was dried blood, and a chill ran through her.

Hold On took the lead of their somewhat straggly line, as he seemed to have the best instincts for water. Estrella soon lagged behind the others at the end of the line. She kept pausing to study the paintings on the rock walls they passed. The humpbacked music maker and his horn fascinated her. She wanted to hear the music he blew. And she kept a sharp eye out for the tiny horse.

Suddenly, there was a shrill whinny. Hold On galloped back toward Estrella. She could feel a current of agitation running through the line of horses.

"Follow me!" Hold On said.

Estrella and Hold On shot off, with the others following.

Estrella picked up a scent, and a sense of dread filled her. It was two scents really — that of deer and that of mountain cat. They came to a halt over a small pile of bones. She would always remember how tiny and delicate those bones were. The fragile backbone had been snapped in half.

"It was the mountain cat," Hold On said, his voice brimming with sadness. "But look at the skull — it has the marks of a coyote's teeth."

Estrella flinched. *That bloodstained muzzle!*

"Coyote?" Grullo asked.

"Yes. The big cat left the small bits to the dogs! *Malditos carroñeros*," he muttered. Estrella had never heard Hold On curse, and this was the harshest curse a horse, a grazer, could cast on another animal.

Sky had been listening quietly. He came forward, his ears laid back, his blue eye shining with fear. "Are coyotes like the vultures you told us about in the meadows in the Old Land? Scavengers?"

"Both. They scavenge and they kill," Hold On said grimly.

Estrella shivered. At least the cat was a noble creature, an honest hunter. There was something degenerate about the coyote.

A few tufts of the fawn's tawny coat had caught up in the prickles of a sagebrush and were quivering in the breeze. Estrella closed her eyes. The image of the fawn dancing under feathery white clouds came back to her. Had there ever been a lovelier or livelier creature? And now he was just bones, and somewhere the coyote skulked, fur still stained with the fawn's blood.

All the horses were very quiet. Their heads hung down as if searching for a reason for the little fawn's death. Deep inside, they knew this was simply the way of the land. This was the price for being wild and free. The weak were prey for the strong, the grazers often victims of the meat eaters. One part of Estrella knew this, and yet another part of her called out, *Not fair!* A small, defenseless creature had died, but the world still went on. The sun was shining brilliantly. New grasses were pushing up. The sky was a clear and beautiful blue. But the ground was stained with the blood of the fawn.

CHAPTER 14

The Dawn Horse

The horses moved on. They found water shortly after leaving the bones of the fawn. But after, the water grew harder to find. What grass there was grew short and dry. Tempers grew as short as the grass. Azul had shifted her anger from Estrella to Verdad.

"I just want to make one thing clear," Azul said in the haughty voice she often assumed. "If we find another water hole, I do hope someone will keep an eye on Verdad. He has a way of sneaking up first and drinking the hole halfway down before the rest of us even have a chance."

"I do not!" Verdad protested. "How dare you?"

"Your name means truth, or so Hold On says." Her voice dripped with contempt. "But I'm not sure if you're so truthful."

Estrella was shocked. She laid back her ears, lowered her head, and began to wave it back and forth at Azul.

"Do you have a problem?" Azul asked.

"Indeed I do. You have managed to insult two of our herd in a very short space of time. First Verdad, claiming he takes an unfair share of water. And then you doubt Hold On's word."

"And I might add I doubt you!" said Azul. "You keep leading us north — north to some sort of sweet grass — but why should I believe you know what you're doing? We're going to die out here! There is no water, no decent grass to eat."

Estrella narrowed her eyes. "You're free to turn back. Yes, go back to the City of the Gods. See how many more horses' heads have been cut off."

Angela and Corazón appeared to be seized by tremors.

"Look at them," said Azul with a flick of her black tail. "Those two old mares. They'll never make it."

Corazón now stepped forward. "I'd rather die of thirst with Estrella leading me than see another horse's head cut off by men. Now, young filly, stop this nonsense!"

The word *nonsense* was like a spark on dry tinder for Azul. She laid her ears flat. "Shut up, you old biddy," she snarled.

Corazón's eyes blazed. She lunged at Azul with her mouth open and bit down smartly on the blue roan's flank. Azul howled as much in humiliation as pain. Angela rushed in, wheeled around, and delivered a sharp kick to Azul's other flank. The rest of the horses stood by amazed.

"Don't look so surprised, Hold On," Corazón snapped. "My sire was in the first cavalry of King Carlos, and my dam died in the Battle of Fornovo. I know how to fight. Old biddy, my withers!" She narrowed her eyes and glared at Azul.

Azul went into a deep sulk and not a word was heard from her. The fight seemed to energize the rest of the horses almost as much as a good graze or a long drink of water. Corazón and Angela had broken the tension, for now. But Estrella was worried. What if they didn't find water soon? What if the grass continued to recede. What would they eat? The tough-skinned plants with the sharp spikes would tear up their mouths worse than any bit. The herd followed her on blind faith. What if she failed?

The horses were passing under a soaring cliff wall, and the sun struck the rock ahead at a fierce angle. Flecks of bright crystals sparkled in the sunlight. The rock face seemed almost to tingle. There, in the center of a nimbus of light, was the carved figure of a tiny horse. It was as if the creature spoke to Estrella. *Tell them! Tell them about the first horse. Tell them how the herd shall run free once more.*

"Come, come in close to this rock!" Estrella called to the herd. She looked fierce and stubborn as she stood against the high cliff. The other horses sensed they were going to hear something of vital importance. Even Azul shoved her ears forward and shed her bored and disdainful air.

"Do you see this figure here in the rock wall?" Estrella pressed.

The horses squinted slightly, for the stone seemed to dance with light. "What do you see, Sky?" Estrella asked.

"A tiny horse running. Running very fast."

"You're right." Estrella paused. She hoped she could explain it properly. "I don't lead us. It's this horse who leads us. This is

First Horse, and we are simply following his trail. Do you understand? First Horse was here long before there were any humans, long before there were horses that looked like us. He is the first horse of the New World, and we are here to find our way back to the fields and meadows where he grazed.

"First Horse passed this way. He went without water and without food for days and yet he survived. Survived to become our first ancestor! And we shall survive, too. We just must believe. See how his neck curves. See his hocks. See his perfect head. This is the horse from the dawn of time."

The nine other horses crowded close to peer up at the tiny horse inscribed in the rock wall, sparkling against a field of embedded crystal flecks.

No one said a word for the rest of the day. But as the herd moved forward, they kept the dawn horse fixed in their minds. The idea that something so small had been the start of them all was almost too much to comprehend. It was an idea as big as the sky, as big as the universe and its most distant stars. And yet many of the horses found a comfort in the thought of a universe old and vast enough to create such a long thread of life.

Hours after they left the rock wall, in the engulfing purple light of the dusk, they discovered two good water holes. After they drank their fill, the herd continued on. Soon they came to a small river and waded across it to the other side. They followed the river as it meandered through groves of cottonwood, willow, and tamarack. In the distance, they could just make out a ragged ridge, but as they drew closer, they realized they had unwittingly descended into a canyon. In the failing light, they saw a most peculiar formation in what appeared to be the cliff walls of the canyon.

"What's that?" Estrella asked, tossing her head to the sheer walls, which had several large openings.

"Windows!" replied Corazón.

"You mean like the portholes on the ship?" Sky asked. He rememberd that some sailors had looked at him through round openings when he had been taken aboard the brigantine.

"But they look like windows in a cliff," Grullo offered.

To Estrella, the windows looked like empty eyes staring blindly into the night.

"Who would live in a cliff?" Corazón asked.

"The Once Upons," Estrella said, peering into the cliff's dark eyes.

"She's right!" Hold On nickered. "And there appear to be trails leading up to those windows."

"But the Once Upons are gone," Angela said. "The deer family told us that."

"Yes," Estrella said softly. She began to quicken her pace.

"Where are you going?" Arriero asked.

"This is their place; this is where the Once Upons lived in the long ago." She could tell the others were agitated.

"Estrella, listen to me," Hold On said. His ears were laid back, and his coat twitched. "I — I — I don't think it's a good idea to go in there."

"Why not?"

"This might have been their city! You know what cities are like. It's all death."

But Estrella shook her head. "No. You're wrong. The Once Upons were before the new men, before the Ibers. They — the Once Upons — were more . . . more . . ." She stammered for a moment. "More wild. More like the little horse on the crystal wall. They were the Originals. This is not a city of death. It's a spirit city."

"Don't go," Hold On said again. "Wait until morning and then I'll go with you."

Estrella nodded reluctantly and joined the rest under a small stand of willows where they would sleep for the night.

CHAPTER 15

The Spirit City

It had been a long day, and the colts had lain down on the powdery dirt under the tree to sleep. The rest locked in their legs for standing sleep and soon their heads were nodding. But not Estrella.

She shifted her weight from one hip to the other. She tried reengaging the joints in her forelegs, then her hind ones. She thought flies were nipping at her and swished her tail half a dozen times at nothing. There were never flies at night. The tiny figure of the horse danced so lively in her brain that sleep was impossible.

Her gaze kept drifting toward the spirit city. She wondered if there would be more carvings up there.

A rising moon bathed the rock dwellings in an eerie glow, but the windows stared out blankly. A thick cloud passed over the moon, nearly quenching it. The cloud hung for some time like a scrim, filtering the moon's light so the city was dappled in silvery gray shadows. Sometimes a wind came along, combing the cloud into strands so thin that they were almost transparent.

The strands seemed to play with the light, as if daring the moon to shine its brightest.

Something sprang from the deepest shadows of the cliff dwellings. Estrella blinked. It swirled out of a window like one of the outlier whirlwinds of a dust storm, but unlike dust, it appeared to sparkle.

The rest of the herd was still sound asleep. Estrella took a step forward. A branch cracked under her hoof, and Hold On flinched and swished his tail. Estrella stopped, waited, and then moved on. She walked slowly, setting her hooves down as softly as possible. It was not easy to move silently. She was no longer the same filly; she'd grown heavier on the grasses they'd grazed. She had grown stronger and faster as well.

She watched the dark windows from which the sparkling whirlwind had jumped. Several times, she thought she saw a shimmering cone of light and with it came a thin, reedy sound. The glow reminded her of the sun ponies the herd had seen on the morning of the mountain cats. Should she be afraid? The sun ponies were meant to bring good luck, but they had brought only bad things — the mountain cats, like the one that had killed the fawn, and the coyote that had picked the skull clean. Estrella felt a shudder pass through her.

The light appeared to beckon her, as if to say, *Come, come, horse, don't be afraid.* Estrella flared her nostrils and blew softly toward the light, then peeled back her lips and sniffed the air.

The only scent she caught was the pungent fragrance of sage-brush cutting the night. As she drew closer, the light seemed to steady, even glow. It settled in a large window near the ground, and a liquid sound drew her closer. The sound, so faint before and louder now, flowed through her. She felt it as one might feel a dream, except that she heard it so strongly, felt it all the way down to her bloodstream. Her own heart seemed to beat the rhythm of the sound.

In one opening in the cliff dwelling, the light glowed deeper and turned to a tawny golden hue like a dawn mist. Did the mist have a shape? The sparkling light began to shift, then dance in the darkness. Estrella stepped across a threshold. A soft breeze stirred the air, and the mist swirled and took form. Suddenly, there was a dewy fawn glimmering before Estrella, dancing and skipping, sometimes bucking, sometimes prancing on its hind legs.

Fawn? she asked.

Yes. I never thought you'd come.

I hear you, but there is no sound.

That's lucky. We wouldn't want to wake the rest of your herd.

But how can this be? How are we speaking with no sound?

It's spirit language, the fawn replied.

I'm not a spirit. I'm not dead. You are. I saw your bones.

Oh, those bones, the fawn said dismissively.

How can this be?

The Once Upons like you the same way they like me. They are drawn to you.

The Once Upons are here?

Of course they are. You said so yourself. They heard you tell the other horses that their spirits were here. The fawn tipped his head, beckoning Estrella. *Follow me.*

Estrella gasped, for a wall suddenly loomed ahead that revealed a herd of tiny figures. *Horses!* And they looked just like the one she had seen in the wall with the crystals.

Indeed! said the fawn. *Tiny, tiny horses — smaller even than fawns like myself.*

Estrella suddenly began to tremble. The fawn sensed her fear.

There are only stories here, he said. *Stories of first creatures. Creatures as they were when they entered the world, before men killed them or rode them or herded them. Stories from when men were as free and as wild as we are.*

It was as if the pieces of a puzzle were falling into place. Estrella wondered what would have happened if the herd had not stopped by the rock wall with the crystal horse that afternoon. Would she have found this city of spirits?

Estrella followed the fawn as he led her deeper into the rooms and winding pathways of the cliff dwellings. Music seeped from the walls, blending into a soft symphonic sound that swelled in the darkness like a night-blooming flower.

Where are we going? Estrella asked.

Wait. You'll see.

But you're blind. How can you see to lead me?

The little fawn made a puffy sound that sounded like laughter. *I can see now!* And two bright little sparkles where his eyes would be began to scintillate.

They had been following a path that wound through several connected dwellings. They passed tables with bowls in which grain had been ground and left as if ready and waiting to be eaten. There were tools in one corner waiting for the hands of a Once Upon, and water dippers as well as lovely bowls and pitchers with intricate designs.

They left everything, Estrella whispered.

Spirits need little, the fawn replied.

Soon, they had entered a large circular room. Estrella was suddenly confused. She thought she had been following the fawn on a spiraling path that led down into a region beneath the earth, but now it felt as if she had climbed through a hole in the night and emerged onto a shimmering plain made of stars. She felt herself wrapped in the radiance of a pearly light. It was almost as if she were on a border between time and place. *Where am I?* Her hooves were buried in a dust of stars that swirled up to her hocks.

Suddenly, there came the wonderful fragrance of the wind grass, the sweet grass. A small herd of tiny horses, much smaller than the fawn, danced across the luminous dust. Even the tall-est of them hardly came up to Estrella's knees.

Estrella stood very still, watching the dance of the spir-its. And as she watched, an overwhelming sense of peace came to her. Shoals of stars washed against dark. Swaths of silvery light undulated like the manes and tails of wild horses tearing across a strange landscape. She wished the tiny horses would dance closer to her, but they kept just out of reach.

Why don't they come close? Estrella asked.

You are so big compared to them.

I'd never hurt them.

They don't know you yet. You're so like them, but at the same time unlike them. Half strangers to one another.

It was as if Estrella were peering at these creatures over a stretch of time as vast as any sea.

Estrella felt a need to tell the little horse in her mind's eye her story. *Little horse,* she said to the figures before her, *I smell the wind grass as my dam did. I saw an image of you flash in my dam's eye before she died. I feel wrapped in the light of her silvery coat. Am I on the right path to find the sweet grass, the wind grass? Am I going where I am meant to be?*

I cannot tell you that, said one of the little horses. *I can only know where you came from. You have to look up to look down.*

Look up to look down? I don't understand. Where are we going?

That is for you to find out, said the little horse. *You are the leader of the first herd.*

Estrella was almost desperate now. She wanted to ask more about the wind grass and the original herd, but the little horse began to dissolve like dewdrops in the morning sun, and soon he and the fawn were gone.

CHAPTER 16

Little Horse

"Why are you mumbling to yourself?" Azul nudged Estrella's flank with her head. Estrella shied and bumped into Hold On.

"What's going on here?" Hold On snorted somewhat grumpily.

Estrella looked around. How did she get back? An eyeblink before, she had been in the spirit city with the little horse and the fawn, and now she was back with the herd. She had no recollection of leaving the spirit city.

"Where are they?" she whispered.

"Oh, for the sake of the Virgin, she's mumbling again," Azul said.

Hold On nipped Azul on the shoulder. "We don't do that here."

"Do what?"

"Swear by the Virgin. We are in the New World now. We don't have bits crammed in our mouths, our heads forced into harnesses. We are not saddled. We forget all that along with the Iber gods."

"But Estrella was mumbling all night!"

"I couldn't have been. I wasn't here," said Estrella.

Hold On blinked, for he could have sworn she had stood sleeping beside him all night.

"Where were you?" Hold On asked.

"I went to the spirit city," she said.

The other horses snorted and gasped.

"You did?" Verdad asked, clearly impressed.

"Why didn't you take me?" Sky seemed nettled.

"You were all too scared to go. I went."

"You went and came back loco," Azul said.

"Here. Here." Hold On stomped his hoof. "No name-calling."

Azul walked off toward a clump of buffalo grass to graze, muttering to herself. "Name-calling! I just call things the way I see them. The filly's crazy. That's all."

They left the spirit city, but they ran into more and more carvings of the tiny horse as they traveled. Estrella found this reassuring. Although the scent of the sweet grass sometimes grew faint, she now felt certain she was following in very ancient footsteps. The other horses walked right by the rock pictures without noticing the tiny herds. It began to irritate her.

"Stop!" she said one day. How could they ignore the carvings?

She'd stopped in front of a picture that was particularly lovely. Tiny horses were almost prancing across the stone face, as if they were dancing to unheard music.

"Why?" Azul asked. "There's water ahead. I'm thirsty."

"Me too," said Verdad.

"What do these look like to you — these pictures in the rocks?"

"Pictures?" Azul said, her voice tinged with contempt. "They look like scratchings."

"Not in the least!" Hold On replied, coming up to them. "They have four legs. The shape of their heads . . . they could be —"

"Horses? Right?" Estrella said.

"No! Wrong!" Azul said. "Look how tiny they are. They're more like ants."

"Big ants?" Corazón offered.

"They're not ants," Grullo protested. "Ants have more than four legs. I've seen enough in my time. These are like the horse that Estrella showed us on the crystal wall. Just not as sparkly."

"Well," Azul said, her voice dripping with disdain, "if they are horses, they are a poor excuse."

"Really, Azul, you think that?" Estrella narrowed her eyes.

Azul laid back her ears. She was larger than Estrella, but she seemed to shrink. "Yes," the roan replied. The other horses had fallen silent.

"Speak for yourself!" Estrella added cryptically. "You saw that horse in the crystal wall. I told you —"

"You told us a story you made up!" Azul interrupted.

"I didn't make it up!"

"You dreamed it or something. All that nonsense about us being led here! I ask you now" —.Azul swung her head to the other horses and flicked her ears — "has any one of you, a single horse here, seen a 'tiny horse' hoofprint? We're following a stupid horse's stupid dream, and she thinks she can be our leader. She has no more right to be our leader —"

Estrella gave no warning signs, no laid-back ears, no lowering and shaking her head. She just charged, slamming into Azul's flank and knocking her onto her back.

"Stop it!" Hold On roared, and raced in between the two fillies. "No more!"

Corazón stepped forward toward Azul, who had scrambled to her feet.

"Azul," Corazón said quietly. "What do you believe in? The Ibers, the Seeker? The men who cut off Centello's head?"

"I believe in truth!" said Azul, her ears so flat they almost disappeared. "I've seen no hoofprints. That is the truth. How can a horse no bigger than a small dog survive? How did it make its way through this new world? How can she know the past?" Azul tossed her head toward Estrella.

Corazón snorted. "You think leadership is all knowledge, do you? Well, it's not. It's also imagination. Knowledge has

limits. Imagination doesn't. Imagination fits this new world."
With that, the old mare turned and walked away.

The horses looked in wonder at the old mare. What she
had said moved them profoundly, especially Estrella. The support from Corazón, who had been so unsure at first, galvanized
Estrella.

As the pack traveled on, Estrella developed as sharp a sense for
water as Hold On. Not just for water but for the best grazing.
And although her mind often wandered back to the spirit city,
she was always alert to the slightest danger.

Nevertheless, Hold On felt that Estrella seemed to have
slipped away from the herd. She often nickered to herself and
he would see her twitching in her sleep. He could not help but
wonder about her dreams. He felt more sure than ever that
Estrella, like her dam, had an old eye and that she was not
simply leading them across the terrain, but leading them into
her dreams. It was as Corazón said — intelligence was not
enough in this harsh terrain. One had to have imagination,
and imagination foaled dreams.

And as far away as Estrella sometimes seemed, Hold On
didn't worry about her. He was much more concerned with the
blue roan. Azul had become not just challenging and cantankerous but bitter. He caught her sly looks at Estrella and it
disturbed him. He saw her sidling up to Angela to nicker in her

ear, and watched Azul's eyes as she cast them toward Estrella. She was obviously gossiping.

But when he really became anxious was when he saw her edging up to Bobtail. It was interesting that she chose Bobtail, and not Grullo, for her whispers. Grullo was smarter, but Bobtail, although not dumb, wasn't nearly as steady. He, like Angela, had been slow to forget the old ways, the old gaits. And of course the bright bay had "the good mouth" so treasured by the Ibers. Sometimes Hold On caught a glimpse of Bobtail making odd motions with his mouth, as if he were searching for a bit. Or perhaps a phantom bit still haunted his mouth. Bobtail could be easily influenced by others, be they humans or horses.

The way Azul clung to her rancor worried Hold On. It was almost a matter of pride for her, as if letting go of her anger would be a sign of weakness. So she nurtured it, tried whenever possible to nettle Estrella. She seemed especially piqued whenever Estrella paused to look at the rock carvings.

"Look at her!" Azul sneered late one afternoon as Estrella approached a carving of three little horse figures. The wind shifted and carried Azul's words directly into Estrella's ears. Estrella wheeled about and charged the blue filly. She reared and pawed the sky just as the stallions had when they defended the herd against the two mountain cats. Azul was not intimidated.

"Looking at your ants again?" Azul taunted. She wheeled about and charged Estrella. The other horses gasped, but Estrella stood her ground as the blue roan barreled toward her. Just when Azul was upon her, Estrella shifted back on her hocks and burst forth in a tremendous leap. She leapt straight over Azul, striking down an angry hoof on the highest point of the blue roan's rump. The blow was not hard, but it was completely unexpected. The blow smarted, but Estrella hadn't drawn blood. Still, Azul was deeply embarrassed. She had charged and somehow Estrella had turned the situation around. The other horses stood stunned.

Estrella trotted by. "Just something I can do with one of my six legs — is that the number ants have? I've never really counted."

Grullo blinked. "Dunno, but I never saw an ant with a hoof."

This broke the tension and several horses snickered.

Azul skulked off, but Estrella was not done with her. She followed. "What do you want now?" Azul wheeled around.

"I'm sorry if I hurt you," Estrella said.

The other horses crowded near to hear.

"I asked what you want."

"I want you to stop!" Estrella paused. "Stop with your poison or leave the herd." She tossed her head toward Hold On and Sky, who were standing closest. "We are a herd. We are as solid as the rock walls of this canyon, as steady as the earth and the ground we set our hooves on. Some of us have been tested in ways you never were. We were cast into the sea with deadly sharks and we swam. Sky was nearly blinded by the lash of a crocodile's tail, and Corazón licked away the blood from his wound."

Azul opened her mouth as if to speak, but Estrella forged onward. "Yet we came through all that. I, who had never set hoof to earth, survived. Corazón, Angela, Hold On. Sky, who had barely galloped before he was led aboard that ship — we survived together. We survived when the Ibers became too thirsty to share their water. We swam when they thought we would drown. We ran and galloped in ways men never dreamed, fought off mountain cats and swamp creatures, and even survived when men tried to kill us and kill one another."

Estrella was trembling now. "We will face more danger together. We know that. But these dangers should not foal from within our own herd. After all we've gone through, it can't be jealousy and greed that destroy us. Humans destroy one another. We are a herd! We have a genius for this new land, this new world. I believe it. I truly believe it!"

CHAPTER 17

To Be Owned?

The air had turned cooler and the nights crisp. The sky seemed to burn with stars. The North Star blazed brighter than ever and the sweet grass scent that so often seemed elusive became stronger.

Azul had not been as surly lately. But somehow this had not set Estrella's mind at ease. She felt as if the air was heavy with Azul's pent-up wrath, the way it was before a summer storm.

Despite the tension, there were undeniable pleasures to be found as they traveled. The seasons were one of Estrella's delights. In the ship, there had been only two seasons — storm or calm, always in heat and darkness. The farther north the herd traveled, the more they were aware of the weather changing. The huge blizzard that now seemed so long ago had been a late spring storm. It was followed by days of scorching heat sometimes broken by terrifying electrical storms where the skin of the sky would peel back to reveal its cracking bones.

Estrella knew now that she had not been fated to pass her entire life suspended in a sling in the hold of a ship. At some point, she would have become part of the world — the human's world. She would have been trained to ride into combat, or to pull a cart, or perhaps just to be ridden by her owner in the countryside. The good days would have been when she was set out to pasture to graze. If she had foaled, and if the foal had been born with straight legs and good hips and an elegantly curved neck, it would be sold, perhaps taken far away.

It was a strange world. Estrella found it difficult to comprehend that Angela sometimes went on about her previous owners. Angela took pride in the men who had owned her and often talked how she could adjust her gait and her ways — *muy elegante* — for her rider. She said she was known to be good with children, but did she never think of the colts and the fillies she had foaled? When Estrella asked her once about her foals, she only commented on how much money her master had received for them. Corazón was a little more sensible. She remembered the family that had owned her but did not hold them in quite the same reverence that Angela did.

One night, when they had settled under the spreading branches of a grove of piñon trees, Estrella asked Hold On if he had memories of his owners.

"Oh, there have been so many, I can't possibly remember them all."

"Do you ever try?"

"No, why should I?"

"Were they cruel?"

"No, no. Not at all. I just don't care to remember that time. We were owned. It is an unnatural state to be owned. I never knew how strange it was until I was free."

Estrella shivered. "What was it like?" she asked in a low voice.

"It means that you have the bit in your mouth even when you don't. It's as if the bit is in your brain. You're never required to think because your master's hand controls that bit that moves your head. It erases any possibility of original thought. His spurs, his reins, the bit — those became your only brain."

"But what about the meadow? Meadow wisdom?"

"You don't wear a bit when you're in the meadow, but you know it's coming. It's as dependable as the moon and the stars. For many, grazing begins to feel like a poor substitute for the grain in our feed bags. You get glimmerings of freedom in the meadow, but it's confusing, even frightening. It's like a sad promise of what could be but never will."

Estrella closed her eyes and thought back to the time she'd spent in the sling. She thought about the dim light in the narrow stall and began to understand what being owned truly meant. The chain they'd put across her gums in the City of the Gods was the closest she'd ever come to having a bit in her mouth. And that was awful enough. But the sling that left chafe marks on her sides and kept her from touching her dam was, in a sense, its own kind of bit. It had been imposed by men to remind her that they owned her, even though she had been foaled by her dam. That was ownership!

Estrella slept badly that night. She had dreams of being lashed with reins, dreams of the bit pulling her neck, pulling her down. Even when the little horse galloped across her mind, it didn't calm Estrella.

Little horse! Estrella called. *Where are you going?*

I'm a horse of the very dawn. I can bring you only partway, if at all. I cannot do everything. You are late to this new world.

As she spoke, Estrella felt the shadow of a coyote slinking closer, coming to chase the little horse away.

Tell me what to do! Estrella begged.

You know, said the little horse. *You see the way.*

Suddenly, the horse quivered, nostrils flaring and ears pitched forward. *The fire winds! Beware! The fire winds begin to blow!*

Estrella felt a soft breeze against her cheek, oddly warm. The wind began to blow harder and hotter, darkening, billowing with smoke and ash. Embers flew at her and nipped at her coat, stinging and burning. Estrella could hear a great roar of flame approaching, the taunting yip of a coyote ringing out above it. The last thing she remembered before she awoke was the little horse engulfed in fire.

CHAPTER 18

Pego

In a distant valley, a dark, handsome stallion followed by a filly and two mares stopped for the night in a grove of piñon trees. He wanted to go on but knew that the younger of the two mares, Bella, was in foal with his colt or filly. He wouldn't risk her.

The three horses weren't far from the City of the Gods when a scent came to him. A blood scent that stirred him deeply. The mare, Bella, carried his foal, but he began to perceive another scent out there as well. The distant scent of a half-grown filly with a blood like his own — the blood of the great desert horses, the Barbs, and the Arabians. He was a *Pura Raza*, a pure-blooded horse, bred for stamina and speed. He was the very best that the two ancient lines could produce, and thus he had been named for the winged star horse in the sky, Pegasus. His owner had whispered the name in his ears as he progressed through his training in the four-beat gaits when he was just a colt. His master, Don Arturo, was a smallish man with crooked legs, but an excellent rider.

The stallion had nursed in his earliest days in a meadow, drinking the milk of the *Pura Raza* of Andalusia. With that milk came the scent, the blood scent, of his desert ancestors. Now the scent seemed to press in upon him with an almost unbearable intensity. It was in the belly of the mare next to him and yet out there in this alien landscape as well. The elusive blood scent of another he had sired.

The stallion had been right to break away from the Chitzen. Nothing had gone well in his life from the day when Don Arturo sold him and he had gone off across an ocean with Don Esteban, who knew nothing of horses.

They had landed on First Island, then followed the path of the Seeker. Pego's owner had one thought: to get the gold before the Seeker.

But there had been delays, and when they arrived, they found themselves with bloody tracks to follow. The Chitzen had stopped worshipping horses as gods, had discovered that horses were more useful than gods. And Don Esteban had · traded Pego, the two mares, and the filly, for gold.

The Chitzen knew nothing about horses. They cared nothing about learning to ride them. They were blind to the four-beat gaits, or the *paso fino*, the fine smooth gait for which the purebloods were known. All they cared about was dragging the horses into their fields to haul a plow like oxen. They were using Pego, the mares, and the filly as common farm animals. They would break his back. When he was able to sire another offspring, it seemed like a miracle to him. And the moment he was sure that Bella carried a foal, he decided they must leave.

The other horses were reluctant, scared, but he had thought it through. He had sensed that the fibrous braided tethers were not as strong as the Ibers' ropes. One moonless night, when the clouds gathered thickly and drained the sky of any light, he began chewing on the braid that tethered him. Within a short time, he had nearly broken through. He whinnied softly.

"Look! Look, what I've done!" The three other horses began to chew. When they had almost cut through, Bella turned to him.

"But, Pego, where will we go?"

"Where our foal will not be treated like an ox! Where our foal will know its true blood, the blood of the great horses of the desert. Now hurry, before the moon comes back."

He needn't have worried, for it was a festival and the Chitzen were deep in their gourds, filled with a liquor that made them stumble. Pego and the others jumped the corral fence without anyone noticing. They disappeared into a pelting rain that had just begun to fall. With each pounding beat of Pego's hooves and with the roar of his heart pumping the blood of his ancestors, he repeated to himself, *I am Pegasus, the God of Horses.* It felt as if he were flying through the slanting rain.

The horses had emerged out of the swampy coastland onto the parched plains and continued north, many days before. He had found the star that never moves, but better, he found the horse constellation for which he was named. It rose each night in the east, its wings thrashing the dark. He learned each of its stars and navigated his way north. Between the blood scent he had picked up and the stars, he would meet his destiny. Of this he was certain.

And so, many days later, Pego and his companions found themselves sheltering for the night under a piñon tree. The night air was crisp, a welcome relief after the heat of the day. The mares rested comfortably, but a slight noise roused Pego. In the distance, he could just make out a line of figures picking its way across the hills. The figures were four-legged, not unlike the deer they'd seen a few days earlier.

The blood scent became stronger, and Pego's ears twitched. But he would wait to approach. Bella needed to rest. Pego would do nothing to risk his unborn foal.

CHAPTER 19

Encounter

Hold On was the first to spot the other horses. He neighed and Azul looked over. The filly seemed to freeze. Her legs locked, and her ears sprang forward. It was just morning, the sun barely edging over the horizon, but the herd could clearly see a figure like a scrap of midnight in the distance. Soon the whole herd was alert to the approach of three horses led by a handsome black stallion. They were transfixed by the newcomers — the first horses they had seen in months.

They are horses — but why do they move in this odd manner? wondered Estrella. They pranced in a way that looked like one of the old gaits yet was slightly different.

Trouble! Hold On laid back his ears.

Corazón stretched out her neck and lifted her head to better see the newcomers. There was something comforting about the way they approached. *What is it . . . ? Ah, a paso fino tiempo doble! And what a lovely double time it is!*

Angela sighed softly and wondered if she still remembered the steps.

Arriero and Grullo twitched their ears, lifted their muzzles, and peeled back their top lips to test the air. They knew that scent — it was a stallion with whom they had shared a pasture briefly on First Island.

Him! They could even smell the scent of Don Esteban, his old master. The god stallion, they had called him scornfully. And like Hold On, they both had a single thought: *Trouble!*

Azul darted out from beneath the cottonwoods, and two squeals pierced the air.

"My filly!" Pego reared and the two raced toward each other. Soon the sire and his filly were nuzzling and inhaling the blood scent that bonded them, the blood scent that had stirred in the shadows of their minds for days.

The first herd remained quiet and observed the reunion. It was rare even in the Old Land that a sire and his foal ever met. Corazón and Angela both had tears trembling in their dark eyes.

Pego looked up and snorted abruptly. "Where do you come from? Where do you go?"

Hold On stepped forward. "We're here."

Pego blinked and cocked his head. *Impudent!* "I know you're here! No games with me."

Arriero tossed his head toward Grullo. "You know us," he said. "We were all on First Island together — all except the young ones. We came on the Seeker's ships to find the Golden One."

"And we're here now, as Hold On said," Grullo answered. "That's all that matters."

"Hold On." Pego turned his head sharply toward the stallion. "Is that a name? I don't call that a name."

"Then don't call me," Hold On answered patiently.

"Who named you that?"

"I named myself."

Estrella stepped forward. "And I am Estrella, but that was not the name the Ibers gave me."

"I'm Sky," called the colt.

"Verdad," said the other colt.

"And I am Angela." Angela looked at Pego nervously, because she, too, remembered him from First Island.

"No, no!" said Pego. "Not with those spots on your nose. You were called the Ugly One, Fea."

"No more," Angela replied meekly.

"We have new names in this new world," Hold On said, ears flattening. "You can name yourself."

The dark stallion's withers flinched. "I was named Pego by my first master. I was named for the sky god. I am Pegasus. I need no other name!"

A single cold star remained in the early morning sky.

The old scent of the sweet grass stirred in Estrella's mind. "We need to go. We rested here nearly all night."

"But you have no shoes!" said Pego. "What happened to your shoes?"

"I might ask you," Grullo said, "why you still have yours."

"We have lost some," admitted Bella. "But we try to be careful."

"Careful?" Hold On replied. He was stunned. "Careful? That's not being careful. This is no country for metal shoes. You'll never feel the earth, the terrain. It changes all the time."

Pego's three companions looked at the dark stallion. They seemed bewildered and slightly doubtful, as if perhaps this old gray stallion with the odd name was right, sensible in ways they had never before considered. Tension loomed in the air.

"Well, suit yourself," Hold On said, hoping to dissipate the strain that enveloped them like a sticky web.

Pego snorted as if to say, I *always suit myself, you fool.*

Estrella started off.

"The filly leads?" Pego said. "Why does the young one lead?"

Estrella kept going, but Hold On stopped and turned to Pego. There was no way to explain anything to the arrogant Pegasus, whose bloodline made him look only back and never forward. How could Hold On make clear that Estrella's bloodline and her heart would guide them to a future in the New World? Hold On merely gave Pego a level look and said, "She leads. We follow. Go where you want."

But of course Pego did not leave. He followed, with the two mares and the filly trotting behind him.

For several days they traveled. An uneasy silence settled upon them. Estrella felt the disapproving eyes of the new stallion like burrs sticking to her haunches. But she was learning to ignore it. Occasionally, she would hear the clink of a metal shoe dropping, followed by a reprimand from Pego to his mares to walk more carefully. She felt sorry for the mares. They seemed so docile, so submissive in a way she was unaccustomed to.

Except from her brief life on the ship and what Hold On and the elder horses had told her, Estrella did not know much about the ways of men. Yet in a strange way, she sensed that Pego felt himself to be a master, like the Ibers. Yes, that was it. He wasn't a leader but a master. He was an extension of the Ibers' bit — a kind of living, breathing bridle.

Estrella had not seen any carvings by the Once Upons since Pego and his horses had joined them. But on more than one occasion, the herd had spied the shadowy profiles of coyotes slinking out of gullies or through thick brush. It made them all quite anxious. All except Pego, who seemed almost captivated by the sly invaders.

"Are they fox dogs like the ones in the Old Land? Their pelt is a different — a different color."

"Their teeth are the same," Arriero said grimly.

"You're scared of them," Azul sneered. She was enthralled by her father, and always traveled close to him. She was becoming more critical of Estrella and the herd. Pego, too, seemed to grow prouder and more cantankerous with each passing day. He still pranced about in his dainty *paso fino* and *andadura*. So far, he was the only horse who had not lost a single shoe. Of this he was inordinately proud, indeed vain. Occasionally, he would deliver short lectures on the importance of keeping the old ways of the Old Land.

Estrella wanted to burst out and say, "We don't need shoes! We don't need men. We don't need bits or bridles — we're free! We're wild!" But she clamped her mouth shut and kept moving forward.

Although it was now approaching autumn, the weather became confused. Some mornings, it was chilly, and then later the same day, fiercely hot winds would blow. Estrella was not sure where they came from. They had been, she thought, moving into a colder season and there were even sometimes little snow flurries and patches of snow on the ground, but then she'd feel a gust of hot wind. The snow patches would melt quickly, and suddenly the weather would turn cool again. The sun was setting earlier and earlier and darkness falling more quickly.

"Wind wars," Hold On said. "We're squeezed between the mountains and the desert we passed through a moon cycle or more ago. The winds from each begin to fight on the edges of the season. Summer does not want to leave, and autumn and winter are eager to come. And so they fight. But summer will tire. There will be one last blast from summer. Recall the blizzard so many moon cycles ago?" Estrella nodded. "That was winter's last stand before spring."

One evening, they stopped along a shallow river bordered with cottonwood. The leaves had turned bright gold. Against the horizon on the other side of the river, blue mountains rose in the distance. Soon a moon would climb over those mountains and spill its silver onto the river. The horses were settling down. Bella, the mare in foal, lay down to sleep, Pego next to her. Azul stood close by with her legs locked. Hold On also had lain down, which was unusual for him. The ground was cooler, Estrella supposed. She peered at a rock at the base of a nearby cottonwood tree for any sign of the tiny horse, but there was nothing. Had he abandoned her? Was there no one left to guide this first herd?

A soft snore came from Pego. In his recumbent position, she could see the gleam of his shoes. He was so proud of those. But with or without them, he would still be a horse with the bloodlines of the Jennets and the Barbs, those Arabian ancestors about which he was so vain and spoke so often. As if he were the only one who shared those bloodlines. They all did, according to Hold On.

What a peculiar creature Pego was.

CHAPTER 20

A Trickster Comes Calling

Pego stirred in his sleep as dry lightning flared behind a herd of thick clouds. He was soon awake and, rousing himself, wandered off a short distance. The lightning sheeted an eerie silence across the sky. A shadow stirred in a bush, and the stallion shied. It was a coyote. The fox dog reared up on its hind legs, and for just a second, it took on the aspect of Pego's old master Don Arturo with his crooked legs, the man who had named Pego for the star god.

Pego was fascinated by the creature before him. The rest of the herd was frightened of coyotes, but not he. Between his star god in the sky and this crafty fellow, Pego felt in good company.

"How can you go wrong?" the coyote said, seeming to read Pego's mind.

"You spoke?" asked Pego. "I thought you were an Iber, my old master. What happened?"

"Ah, a trick of my trade! You can be a master, too. A master of this herd."

Pego's ears pricked up. "Who are you?"

"I am Coyote. Some call me First Angry."

"That's a strange name."

"It is indeed. It doesn't fit. You can't be angry and do what I do. You have to be calm to think."

"What exactly do you do?" Pego asked.

"You'll see. Stick with me, horse. I can slip through anything."

"Stick with you to where?" asked Pego. He kept one ear toward the coyote and turned the other to the sleeping herd behind him.

"Deep into the canyon where the shade cools. Lead them in and I shall then lead you out — out of fire, out of death. Out as master!"

Dawn tinted the horizon, and a slight wind wrinkled the surface of the river. The wind was warm, too warm for this early in the morning, this late in the year. As soon as Estrella awakened, she felt empty, as if the world had turned hollow. She walked down to the banks of the river and peered at her reflection. Her face had changed. Her head was different, longer. She still had a star on her brow, but it was partly obscured by the long black forelock that flopped down between her ears. But it was her legs that amazed her. She waded in a bit so she could see more of her reflection, and wished her dam were here to see how she had grown. Her legs seemed so long and the white "stockings" had grown with them. It was an odd word, *stockings*. Estrella recalled a conversation she had had with her dam once.

"What are stockings, Mamita?"

"They are clothes the Ibers wear on their feet."

"But, Mamita, these are not clothes! These are my feet, my legs, my coat. Why do they call them stockings?"

"Because it is the Ibers' world, and they are the namers."

Estrella had accepted that then. But now they were in this new world and they were free. They did not wear saddles or bridles or the iron shoes of which Pego was so proud. Just then, she heard the clink of Pego's shoes on the stones of the river-bank. He turned his head toward her and nodded respectfully.

"Still the hot wind blows!" Pego said.

"Yes," Estrella replied.

"I hope you don't feel that I am intrusive," he said in a gentle tone that Estrella hadn't heard from him before.

"Yes?"

Pego hesitated. "I understand that you lost your dam. She was killed in a most unfortunate manner."

"Yes!" said Estrella. "We were thrown overboard during a long calm, and a shark —"

"I can't imagine how terrible that was for you."

Estrella stared at the stallion. It seemed as if he had changed overnight.

"I am so fortunate," Pego continued, "to be reunited with my filly Azul at last. You know, I never saw her even as a foal. Her dam and I were separated on First Island."

"That's sad," Estrella said.

He nodded. "But not nearly as sad as what you went through."

Estrella said nothing. She simply could not understand the change in the arrogant Pegasus.

"I — I . . ." He hesitated, even seemed to falter slightly. "Look, these winds, they're hot. Take it from an old desert horse."

An old desert horse! Pego never referred to himself this way. He made it sound as if he were a nag who had just wandered over.

"I'm not sure how long these winds will blow," Pego continued, "but the heat will wear us down. It'll be cooler if we travel near the river. We'll be near water. And it seems to me that the river might lead into a canyon, which means protection from the hot winds." He paused. "These winds aren't exactly going our way. They're against us."

Our way? Estrella wondered. *Since when has Pego cared about our way?* She was about to say something, but she stopped herself. Pego was being so humble.

He cleared his throat. "I know you and Azul have had your . . . differences. But I always tell her, 'Estrella is the leader. We must follow.'"

At this, Estrella lifted her head and blinked.

"Really!" he said. "There's no horse steadier than old Hold On. He follows you, and he's no fool, that stallion."

"That's kind of you," Estrella said.

She looked down the river. It was like a ribbon of gold in the early morning sun, and yet it was still fairly cool. The winds would come up and it did feel as if the day would grow uncomfortably hot. As Hold On said, the seasons were still fighting, summer stubborn to stay and autumn, winter's outrider, trying to clear the way. She looked toward the bend in the river and saw large shadows splashed across it. If they followed the river and it really did lead into a canyon, they'd be protected from the sun by the shadows of the high sandstone walls. She had to admit it was a good idea.

The herd was just rousing itself. They should leave soon in order to get into the canyon before the sun climbed too high. Estrella turned to alert the others, but she shied and jumped sideways as she caught sight of a fleeting shadow slip out from the trees. "Did you see something?" she said to Pego.

"What?"

"A shadow or, well — I'm not sure. It could have been an animal, maybe even a man!"

Pego nickered softly. "No, I didn't see anything. It was probably just a trick of the light."

CHAPTER 21

The Door in the Mist

Pego was right. The river did run into a long, deep canyon, a shadowy cleft of dappled light. Sometimes the cliffs soared so high that only a blue ribbon of sky could be seen. But there were no carvings on the sandstone. The little horse had vanished and the scent of the sweet grass was fading as well. Estrella tried to conjure up that flash she had seen in the enormous eyes of her dam as she was dying. But she couldn't. She tried to recall the tiny horse figure. All the touchstones that had guided her seemed to be melting away. She had never felt so alone, even with Hold On trotting beside her. And with each step that took them deeper into the canyon, Estrella felt as if she were approaching a profound danger, something she could not understand or control.

Yet Pego had been right. It was cooler.

The river was becoming more shallow. They had swum in its cool waters earlier, but now their feet scraped the bottom. Gradually, it became more a creek than a river, and within a couple of days, it was only a trickle. The trees had grown sparse and the soft sand beaches the horses loved to sleep on thinned away to small strips.

One evening, Pego, the three mares, and Azul slept apart from the rest of the herd on the other side of the trickle where they found a small patch of sand. Bella, whose girth had expanded with the foal she carried, needed a soft place to rest.

"Is her time coming near?" Estrella asked Hold On.

"Not yet. It takes a long time to grow a foal. She is not ready, but it's hard for her and will become even harder."

Hold On looked at Estrella. She had been unusually quiet since they had entered the canyon. "What's wrong, Estrella? Something is bothering you."

She gave him a stricken look. "I think I've lost the way."

"What do you mean?"

"The sweet grass," she nickered, so softly he could hardly hear her.

"Try not to worry. You'll find it again. It will come to you."

The more she thought about the haunting scent, the more elusive it became. And it wasn't just the scent of the sweet grass that was dying away. Ever since they had entered the canyon, Estrella's memories of her dam had begun to fade. She tried hard to bring them back, to recall them, but the only thing she could remember of her time with her dam was the stall door. She began to miss Perlina desperately, yet she could not quite remember what she was missing. The image of her dam started to dissolve, like the figure of the tiny horse.

Estrella could not sleep. Shadows scuttled across the moonlight and she heard the shuddering hoot of an owl. Estrella wandered toward a small clump of a brushy shrub that they had started to call rabbit brush since there were often rabbits around it. The rabbits scattered when the horses approached to graze, but there were no rabbits near this bush. The flowers were more white than yellow, and the bush had a different smell. Still, Estrella was hungry and she nibbled for a while on the slim tender branches with their clusters of fragrant flowers. They were delicious and the more she nibbled, the more she wanted. Her hunger seemed insatiable. Soon she had eaten the shrub down to its roots. She was left with the loveliest thoughts and she felt a soft tranquility flow through her.

A dark shape flitted by. *Coyote?* she thought, not even afraid. She pricked up her ears and decided to follow it.

Two bats swooped through the air. Estrella thought she spotted a small patch of light ahead. As she walked toward it, the patch seemed to glow brighter, as if a piece of the moon had fallen down through the night. The shape of the patch was vaguely familiar to her. *A stall door!* she thought suddenly. But a stall without walls? The door hung in the night between two rabbit bushes. Estrella blinked. How could this be? She was a bit woozy in her head, but the ground felt like ground. She stepped up cautiously and through the door. Would she see the little horse?

Not the little horse, but your own dear dam. A misty figure melted out of the darkness.

Mamita? Estrella was flooded with joy.

Hold On woke suddenly. Something was wrong. The stallion sensed it immediately. Where was Estrella? He got up, found her tracks, and followed them to a shrub with an oddly familiar smell. Estrella had been here grazing, but why would she eat a strange plant down to the ground? Some horses were known to eat odd things when they were disturbed or nervous. Was Estrella truly losing the scent of the sweet grass as she had feared? Hold On was stumped.

Everything seemed upside down. The proud stallion Pego had become much more agreeable, even companionable, and so had Azul. Pego finally seemed to acknowledge that Estrella was the leader of this herd. He would not break away from them, Hold On believed, not until Bella had foaled. It was very possible that after the foal arrived, Pego would leave with his three mares and the new foal to start a new herd. But for now, Pego and Azul were both behaving well. So what was there to bother Estrella?

Hold On continued to follow Estrella's hoofprints. Then he

came upon an unbelievable sight. Estrella was speaking to a coyote, speaking to it as if it were her dam. Suddenly, it all made sense to him. The plant, the one she had eaten to the ground! It was *flora loca* — crazy plant! It grew in the Old Land as well, but horses learned to avoid it because of the strange behavior it caused. But to talk to a coyote! Hold On charged forward.

"Mamita, I've been trying to find you," Estrella said. Her dam's back was to her, and Estrella couldn't see her face. She so wanted to see those dark, reassuring eyes.

"Have you?" her dam replied, still turned away. "Have you really?"

"Of course! But I thought you had left me! I don't understa —"

"Oh, let's not talk about that!" Her dam shook her head dismissively.

"Sorry," Estrella said quietly. Her dam didn't seem to hear her. On the other side of the door, something stirred. Was it the little horse? Estrella wondered, beginning to turn her head.

Her dam wheeled around, her eyes glowing a pale greenish yellow.

Had Mamita's eyes always been that color? Estrella didn't speak out loud, but her dam knew exactly what she was thinking.

"Yes, of course, Estrella! You never noticed, I suppose." Her tone was sharp. Perlina never spoke like that. Never!

The joy Estrella had experienced moments before began to drain away, leaving a terrible hollowness again. Perlina's yellow eyes narrowed, and her lips parted into a hideous grimace.

"Mamita?" Estrella asked, trying to control the trembling in her withers.

A cackle slithered from the creature as her grimace split to reveal a mouth studded with sharp, bloodstained teeth. The creature began to circle Estrella, coming closer each time. But Estrella could not make her legs move. She was rooted to the ground. She smelled carrion breath. Then her dam's head seemed to split again. A new face rose as her dam began to wither away. Estrella shied as the new head, sly and dun-colored, with fresh blood dripping from its muzzle, barked. A coyote reared up before her. The night shredded with its savage yips for fire, for blood.

There was a loud crackle and hot gusts began to rip through the canyon. Grullo gave a piercing whinny, followed by the squeals and shrieks of the herd. Estrella reared and screamed as the coyote lunged at her.

Its eyes glittered with malice. "You thought I was your dam, fool!" The rabbit bush caught fire and flames whipped around them. The coyote rose on his short hind legs and began to dance through the flames untouched. His eyes rolled madly in his head as he sang.

I am coyote,
I am coyote.
I slip and slink
Into your head
So you can't think.
I am the dream stealer,
The fantastic concealer.
Crafty and sly,
I'll sell you lies.
A merchant of death,
I'll swipe your breath.
I am coyote,
I am coyote.
And now the fire winds shall blow!

FIRE

CHAPTER 22

Trapped!

The canyon was engulfed in flames in seconds. Screams filled the air as the horses tore through a sea of fire. Sparks landed on their manes and tails, igniting them. The flames devoured the very air, and Estrella realized she was fighting for every breath. This was death! Stone walls boxed them in, and as they raced away from the heat, a third wall rose in front of them. A dead end! They were trapped in a box canyon.

Hold On was running too fast, and blinded by smoke, he slammed into the rock face. He staggered and choked. His tail had burned off entirely. Estrella's eyes rolled wildly as she scanned the wall for a way out.

A door, you fool? she scolded herself. *Is that what you're looking for, like the dream door that led to this nightmare?* A horse gasped beside her and collapsed on the ground. Was it Hold On? The smoke was too thick to tell. There was a loud crack, and lightning forked through the smoke. In the heat, Estrella experienced an odd sensation. She realized that her hooves were wet. She was standing in a flow of water. The creek was barely a trickle now, not enough to reach past her hooves to the ruff of her coat just above them. So where had this water come from? A new river?

Estrella looked, wheeled around, and spotted a tiny figure, no larger than a dog. It was the little horse, not the carving but a figure that moved and breathed. Had it been unlocked from its stone wall? It seemed to glow in a gauzy light. A jet of flame streaked out behind him, and the little horse turned and beckoned with its head, as if to say, *This way! This way!*

"This way! Follow me!" Estrella whinnied. She galloped toward the tiny horse ahead of her. Just as she reached him, he vanished into a crack in the wall that the smoke had obscured. *The horse is so small! We'll never fit!* She bunched herself up as much as she could and threw herself at the rock.

Estrella stumbled into a cool passageway. The rock walls of the passage were studded with bright crystals, just like the ones on the cliff near the spirit city. But now the figure of the little horse had escaped from the stone and, with its bright white tail, he was easy to follow. She could hear the rest of the herd behind her, their hooves splashing in the tumbling waters of the stream that had carved a way through the rock.

They're following!

Estrella kept her eyes fastened on the tail of the tiny horse, but soon he dissolved into darkness. The crystals of the wall seemed to float out from the rock, and the tunnel grew darker and darker, until all of a sudden, the tunnel widened and the horses found themselves safe, through to the other side, under the comforting black of the night. Then one by one, the crystals began to reappear, suspended in the velvety black of the night. They had become the stars.

Estrella and the horses had emerged into a starlit canyon. They could see the glow of the fire behind them, but brighter still was the star that never moved. The North Star. Estrella heard the horses coughing behind her, some panting in pain. But they were coming. The ground sloped upward. They were climbing out of the deadly river valley they had followed for so many days. Snow spun in the air and for the first time in so long, the air felt cool and crisp.

As they emerged on a high plain, dawn was rising. A bird carved an arc in the pale pearl gray of the sky, a soft gray just beginning to steal across the horizon. Lavender clouds skimmed low along the skyline, like fish swimming in a shallow sea. The stream gushed nearby, and the herd found a grove of piñon tees.

Estrella looked over the herd. They were singed, and some were still coughing violently, but were they all there? Pego, Azul, and the three mares were missing. But she saw Angela, breathing heavily, and counted Corazón and Grullo, Arriero, Bobtail, and the two colts.

A panic welled up inside her. Hold On! Where was Hold On? Had he disappeared with Pego? No . . . no, he'd been beside her near the rock wall!

Something awful shivered through her. And Pego? Where was he? She remembered him from the night before, sleeping away from the others with his mares and Azul. It dawned on her now — the sand was so soft and silent. Pego knew what was coming! He had gotten out with his mares and filly. This was Pego and Coyote's doing! Just as coyotes brought death and chaos, so had Pego brought the forces of destruction down on the herd!

"Where's Hold On?" Corazón whinnied.

"I thought he was right beside me!" Grullo said.

"Did he . . . did he . . . ?" Verdad couldn't complete the thought.

"No! Never!" Estrella whinnied, her voice harsh from the smoke. She coughed violently and her front knees buckled. "He didn't die. Hold On can't die!" Estrella turned furious eyes on the colt.

Angela and Corazón exchanged worried glances. Angela slowly approached Estrella and began to run her muzzle through the filly's singed mane.

"Maybe, Estrella," she began gently, "he's like his name."

"What do you mean?" Estrella cried, frantic eyes on the blaze of fire in the night sky behind them.

"His name is Hold On, and maybe it's his talisman. Maybe that old stallion is holding on."

Corazón came up to her other side and began to nuzzle Estrella softly. "And remember the other meaning of his name, dear. *Espero*, hope. We can hope."

When the herd recovered their strength, they began to stagger through a new terrain studded with rock formations that seemed to lift straight from the ground. It was a country of many shapes, flat-topped rocks, spires, and pillars. It was a land worn by wind and water, polished for eons by the forces of nature into the mystery unique to all things timeless.

The two horses dearest to Estrella had been destroyed, one by water and one by fire. First the dam who had nursed her and then the old stallion who had guided her so faithfully — both were gone and Estrella's chest was tight with grief. Had she been foaled only to endure loss? The world felt empty to her, hollow. Behind her she could hear the smoky gasps of the herd. They were following her, but why? How could she lead without Hold On by her side?

They came to a small pond and waded in to slake their thirst. Their lungs burned still from the heat of the smoke. Estrella stared at her reflection. Part of her forelock had burned away, and her star was obliterated by soot, her mane thick with ashes. Her eyes were red and streaming, and her white stockings had turned gray. *It would have been easier to —*

But she didn't complete the thought. A breeze riffled the water, and the light from the morning sun danced across the dark surface of the pond. She blinked. For a moment, she thought she saw the reflection of a tiny horse leaping the small waves of the pond. Then there was a tendril of a scent — a sweet scent untouched by fire. She lifted her tail and shoved her ears forward. The grass — the sweet grass! How could life and death intertwine so closely? Did the others smell it? No. It didn't matter.

She was the keeper of the scent, the leader of the herd . . . The leader, yet she felt so alone. She had lost so much. First her dam, and now Hold On. But there was still a kindling in her mind like the light of the most distant and ancient stars. Was it a remnant flicker from her dam's eye? For with it came the scent of the sweet grass. She would go on. She would lead this herd, this first herd. She turned her head to the north and felt a tremor pass through her withers. *I have grown strong from my dam's milk. I can go to the farthest edge of this continent. This is my destiny.*

She turned and watched the herd as they drank. Grullo looked up toward her.

He wants to know where we go from here. She whinnied. The others looked up. Estrella began to speak.

"I know you are tired, our eyes still weep from the heat of the fire. Our manes are singed. But remember, we have swum through shark-filled waters. We have leapt over the lashing tails of crocodiles. We have been hobbled, tethered, beaten, tricked into a fiery canyon. And yet we have come out into clear air beneath this starry sky. We are strong. If there are deserts, we shall cross them. If there are mountains, we shall climb them. If there are rivers, we shall swim them. For we . . . we are the first herd in this new world!"

Author's Note

Winston Churchill once said that history is written by the victors. *The Escape* is, in one sense, a novel of alternate history in that it is not being told from the point of view of the victors or the vanquished, but of the horses. In my equine retelling of the coming of horses to the New World, I have conflated certain events and pressed them into a shorter time frame. Here is what is true and what is fiction:

Christopher Columbus discovered America in 1492. However, the key event of what we think of today as the conquest of the New World began nearly thirty years later, in February of 1519, with Hernando Cortes sailing from Cuba to Mexico. This single voyage marked the return of horses to the continent for the first time in tens of thousands of years.

Eohippus equus, or the dawn horse, was considered the very first horse on the North American continent. It was tiny — no more than ten to twenty inches in height. Its evolution began some fifty million or more years ago. This first horse, the dawn horse, survived for several millions of years and became the progenitor of three other species of ungulates, one of which,

Orohippus, continued the horse lineage. The horse evolved through millennia of cataclysmic geological upheavals and changes of climate, as well as shifts in tectonic plates that caused mountain ranges to rise and then buckle, and rivers to carve new courses.

Millions of years later *Mesohippus* horses arrived, and then *Merychippus*. Each successive species became larger and resembled more closely the horse of today. One of the most modern looking, *Equus caballus*, evolved about 1.7 million years ago. It was considered the "true horse" and closest, in terms of its genetics, to the horses Cortes brought to America.

However, *Equus caballus* had disappeared from North America nearly twelve thousand years before Cortes ever reached the continent. Why these first, true horses, the descendants of the dawn horse, left the continent is a puzzle. Some scientists believe the Ice Age drove them north across the Bering land bridge to Asia. Others feel it was human migration south across the same bridge that killed them. In either case, the horse vanished from its original homeland, and it was not until Hernando Cortes decided to conquer Mexico that horses came home, setting foot once again on the soil of their origin. The year was 1519, and these were the horses from which the wild mustangs of the West descended.

Cortes's first stop when he left Spain as a young man was Hispaniola, in 1504. In 1511, he accompanied Diego Velàsquez de Cuellar on an expedition to conquer Cuba. When, in 1519, Cortes set out to explore and conquer the Aztec empire of Mexico, ruled by Montezuma, he sailed with eleven ships, five hundred men, and sixteen horses. In my novel I have not specified how many ships, but I have increased the number of horses to seventeen. Bernal Diaz de Castillo, who accompanied Cortes and wrote the definitive history of the Spanish Conquest, gave names and details of several of these horses. He commented on which ones had "good mouths," and which were steady or skittish. Some of the names that he reported in his writing I have kept — Arriero and Bobtail are real names. Castillo mentioned that a Jewish blacksmith, Hernando Alonso, who was fleeing the Spanish Inquisition, was aboard one of the ships. He also reported that, in one battle, Indians cut off the head of a horse and sent the head around their villages to prove that horses were not gods, but mortal.

The Cortes expedition landed on the Yucatan Peninsula. They advanced to the Aztec capital, Teotihuacan, where they were received peacefully by Montezuma. There, the Spaniards imprisoned Montezuma. Some months later, in the summer of 1520, a rebellion broke out and Cortes and his men had to fight their way out of the city. On this night Montezuma was thrown from a parapet of his own palace and killed. The retreat of Cortes became known as *La Noche Triste*. Some horses escaped and headed north.

Subsequent conquistadors followed, though not precisely in Cortes's tracks, very shortly thereafter or in the following decades. They brought with them more horses and cattle as they began to settle regions of the southwest. Francisco Vasquez de Coronado came into the desolate reaches of Arizona with more than five hundred horses. Juan de Onate brought fifteen hundred horses and mules into New Mexico. Many of these horses died in the early days of the conquests.

There is one story that I found particularly haunting. Deanne Stillman, in her book *Mustang, The Saga of the Wild Horse in the American West*, writes that, contrary to the records, there is a legend "that [a] foal born to [a] brown mare en route from Cuba survived, escaped at some unknown time, and ran toward its ancestors, over mountains and across valleys and canyons and rivers, through cloudbursts and dust storms and days of no water, left to carry on by jaguars and wolves and snakes, perhaps aided by animal spirits, particularly chattering birds that urged the foal onward as it grew older," until it eventually found its own kind.

It is my feeling that fiction often begins where history leaves off.

KL

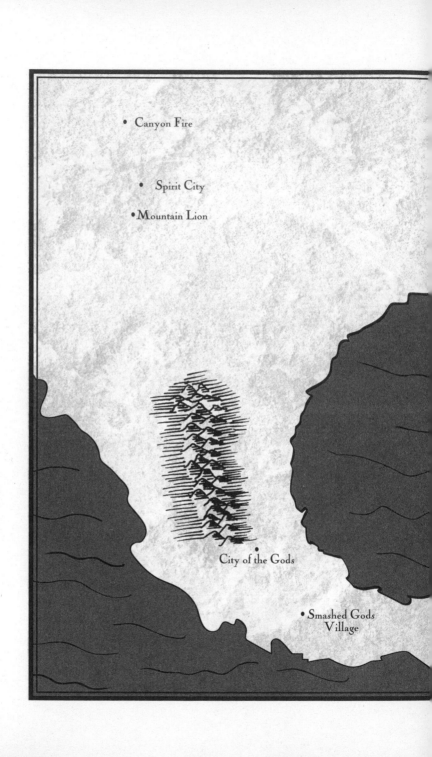

• Canyon Fire

• Spirit City

•Mountain Lion

City of the Gods

• Smashed Gods
Village

Castoff
Island

First
Island